DJ STONEHAM

ALICE FALLS AGAIN

authorHOUSE®

AuthorHouse™ UK
1663 Liberty Drive
Bloomington, IN 47403 USA
www.authorhouse.co.uk
Phone: 0800.197.4150

Published by AuthorHouse 05/14/2019

ISBN: 978-1-5462-9987-5 (sc)
ISBN: 978-1-5462-9988-2 (hc)
ISBN: 978-1-5462-9986-8 (e)

Library of Congress Control Number: 2018913535

Print information available on the last page.

This book is printed on acid-free paper.

This book is dedicated to my parents. To my late mother, Pat, who brought children's stories to life and awoke in me a love for fantasy. And to my father, Don, whose love of nature gave me a boundless environment for my own creations to come alive in.

ACKNOWLEDGEMENTS

Creating this book was mostly pure pleasure (writing), sometimes hard work (editing) and occasionally both at the same time. Can't wait to do it again!

My heartfelt thanks goes to "the team"; Laurel Colless, for the encouragement, advice and sparring you gave me throughout the process; Heather Ross-Sirola for being so professional, positive and honest at the editing phase (you were honest, weren't you?); Juhani Pitkänen, for rescuing my illustration ideas and pulling a rabbit out of a hat (several in fact); the master himself and continued source of inspiration, Charles Lutwidge Dodgson (1832-1898), for discovering Wonderland; and the dedicated group of nursery rhyme researchers.

Thanks to my amazing wife and best friend, Johanna, for putting up with my bizarre ideas and compulsive writing disorder (might not be quite over, dear). My gratitude also to family and friends - you unknowingly keep me sane (well, sane enough); Wayne's Coffee at Myyrmanni shopping centre (for never running out of skinny latte); and my two golden retrievers, for warming my feet and never once being negative about my writing.

CONTENTS

Chapter 1 The Daisy Chain 1

Chapter 2 The Weir-Wolf 23

Chapter 3 Moor Is less... 51

Chapter 4 The Funny Farm.. 77

Chapter 5 All About Town 101

Chapter 6 The Unfair 123

Chapter 7 The Council House 141

Chapter 8 Home Sweat Home 167

Chapter 9 All Ends If Not Always Very Well 193

Index of Nursery Rhymes 219

About the Author 223

If only I could see the way you do.

The perch glided slowly towards Alice, allowing her just enough time to regret not feeding the fish earlier. One, two, three, four, five, once I caught a fish alive.

CHAPTER I

THE DAISY CHAIN

Alice was feeling down. Down where, she wasn't entirely certain but she was sure it wasn't down the rabbit hole again. She'd know if it were. It would be much, much darker.

The sudden thought of Wonderland and those strange places and people she had encountered all those years ago made her stomach churn. She'd been too busy of late to waste time on those memories. But now and again, they crept up on her like ghosts from the shadows, with clammy fingers. She also found herself wondering if strangers were called so because they were strange. It was indeed true of Wonderland but of people in the real world she had too little experience to say for sure. All that was about to change.

Concentrate on what you will pack in your suitcase tonight, she told herself. *Red shoes or blue? Or both?* Black would be the sensible choice, she could almost hear her mother say. *I'll take all three*, Alice decided. One can never have too many shoes. "*Of shoes and ships – and sealing wax ...*" the Walrus said.

1

Truth be told, the idea of returning to Wonderland both fascinated and terrified Alice. It was an impossible combination, rather like jam and gherkin sandwiches. *An oxymoron perhaps*, though Alice wasn't entirely sure. It brought to mind what her two aunts sometimes said about Uncle Percy, who, on returning home from the war, had apparently left a part of himself behind at the front line. That is, in addition to his right leg. Despite his ordeal, Uncle Percy yearned to return to the front line. Alice hoped that he would one day have a chance to search for what he had left there, though she doubted that the line was visible any more.

It was a hot hazy afternoon on a late summer's day. Alice lay by the riverbank, her toes dangling in the cool water, both teasing and terrifying the minnows. They wanted food, probably some white bread and butter, but all they got were Alice's toe jam. At the other end of her body, her hair twined like ivy around the cowslips and the daisies. The air was thick with the scent of meadow and earth, yet not quite masking the faint sweet odour of rotting grass. The low constant hum of honeybees was interspersed with melodies from finches, song thrushes and a solitary blackbird. Yet Alice knew this orchestra was also made up of wasps that stung and blowfly that carried disease.

To tell the truth, which was the only way she told things, Alice knew why she was feeling down. It was because the long summer vacation had come to an end. Schooldays were over for good. Tomorrow, she would leave home and board a train for London to study History at college. She wasn't exactly sure how she felt about this radical change. On the one hand, she was excited by the prospect of a new life. She was fed up with her boring life at home, where one day drifted unnoticed into the next. She was glad to leave behind the household chores, the ignorance that came with being a child, along with the stuffy attitudes of her home tutor and parents. Adults were forever sharing their "wisdom and experience" by ordering her about and dishing out annoying sayings, like "What doesn't kill you makes you stronger". On the other hand, the enormity of the change scared her. Now that she had grown up, she realised there had been a beauty to the innocence of childhood, a carefree existence she would never be able to recapture. Nowadays, she was "expected to know better" and "realise the consequences of her actions". It was funny how they expected her to behave like an adult but still spoke to her as if she were a girl.

Leaving home also meant she would miss things that she had taken for granted; the old house (despite the Chippendale furniture her parents were so obsessed with); her sisters (not so much her brothers); and her ageing cat, Dinah, which she swore talked far more sense to her than any human. She would miss familiar faces. Even that of the good-looking boy at church, who had stared improperly at her while singing Onward Christian Soldiers off-key last Sunday. Living in London would be fraught with challenges, dangers even. Just the notion of it made her heart beat faster.

If she could make no sense of her feelings then they were obviously nonsense and she should focus on the facts. The fact was, tomorrow would be the start of her new life. New places and faces. One of her father's favourite (and most annoying) sayings was: "Look on the bright side." Admittedly, he had said it less of late since contracting a serious disease, though he still put on a brave face and would not hear a word said against Alice going away to study (when his memory didn't fail him). She knew her mother wanted her to stay with the family but who would deny what might be her father's last wish? Alice felt guilty about not postponing her studies. She didn't even know if she wanted to read History. As her sisters said, it was all in the past. There again, her father wanted her to become more independent, be educated and live life to the full. She would therefore try to see the bright side of leaving. Life in London would be exciting. Why, the train journey alone was bound to be an adventure.

Alice had done her homework. She had already learned most of the new London Underground routes and stations off by heart, just in case she got lost in their dark and windy tunnels (Alice was understandably afraid of tunnels). By contrast, the stations sounded like marvellous places, even if some of them were not yet open. Alice imagined that the people at Bayswater and Ealing all had boats and liked fishing; Baker Street must have the loveliest of aromas; Shepherd's Bush must be quite rural, as was perhaps Moorgate: the people of Aldgate were clearly elderly; the inhabitants of Barbican, Cannon Street and Gunnersbury sounded aggressive, whereas the people at Elephant & Castle must be positively batty. She was sure she would like those people most of all.

As Alice was recalling the station names in her head and conjuring up a fanciful picture of London, she heard the piercing whistle of a distant train. It was somehow out of place in the gentle murmur of the summer countryside. It sounded wrong and it startled Alice out of her daydream. The noise was followed by a rustle in the undergrowth nearby. There was no telling if it was a bird, a hedgehog or even a fox. Or something more dangerous that shouldn't be there. Alice knew some of the names of the surrounding plants - green spleenwort, mountain melick and hart's tongue fern – and could easily imagine a wolf or goblin creeping through such menacingly-named vegetation. Or a white rabbit. She shook her head and laughed at herself for being so jittery, while deep down reassuring herself that the creature making those noises had nothing at all to do with Wonderland. As if to answer her fears, a large jackdaw hopped across the meadow and stopped to stare at her.

Would she return to Wonderland given the chance? With all its nonsense and lawlessness? With all the disbelief and torment from her siblings and parents afterwards? Not forgetting the images that still came to her in her sleep. Would she cross the line if invited? Like Uncle Percy?

The train blew its whistle again, a faraway echo, yet so clear one would think it were within arm's reach. This time the noise didn't stop. Alice sat up, her heart beating just that tiny bit faster. Why did the sound linger? As she waited for her head to clear (the head often finds it disagreeable when the body decides to sit up quickly) she caught sight of a movement in the water behind the reeds. A water snake appeared to be winding its way slowly across the surface of the river. Or was it a snake?

Alice rubbed her eyes as one does when something appears to be out of place and looked again. This was no snake. There, about six feet from the riverbank, was a tiny train; a black steam engine with the words "Brighton Express" on the side, pulling a dozen or so carriages along behind it. It was drifting along, though judging by the amount of steam coming out of the funnel, the train seemed to be trying to fight the current.

The spectacle itself was strange enough, yet could have been explained by a boy having dropped his toy train into the river. What was more difficult to comprehend was the sight of tiny heads and arms leaning out of the carriages and faint but desperate cries for help.

The scene was quite beyond belief. And as Alice had first hand experience of what lay beyond belief, she felt inclined to jump up and run home as fast as she could. But Alice was also very curious. And she wasn't the type to walk away from someone in danger, as these poor people clearly were.

Alice jumped up, crouched by the water's edge and leaned forward to take a closer look. Sure enough, there were scores of frightened passengers in the carriages. The more she stared, the more detail she could make out, as if the train were growing larger or she were getting closer to it. It was like looking at something down a telescope, without the telescope.

It unnerved Alice to know that the train was a good six feet away, while simultaneously feeling like it was within an inch of her face. She could see the panic in the people's faces; the fear in their wide-open eyes that said they had no idea what was happening to them or why. Their screams became clearer and she was sure she heard a tiny voice shout "Crazy train!". It was a crazy train for sure.

There was an important decision to be made; whether to run away or try to help those poor people. Alice being Alice meant there was no real choice at all, so grasping a clump of sedge in one hand, she leaned out towards the train. As she focused her eyes on the carriages, she saw that the tips of her fingers were within a few inches of the outstretched hands of the passengers and, somewhat frighteningly, appeared to be the same size. She pushed her face closer still to the train and felt the wind and spray in her face as the locomotive sped across the water. She heard the roar of the steam engine's pistons as they fought the current.

Alice wasn't sure whether it was the shock of touching one of the passengers' hands or the realisation that the sedge had become uprooted from the riverbank. Whichever it was, she became aware that she was falling. Any doubt about where she was falling to was washed away by the sudden and complete change in her surroundings, from warm air and yellow sunshine to a murky green world of ice-cold water.

Knowing the river was barely a foot deep near the bank, Alice tried to stand up on the river bed but her feet only found more water. In fact, the current was so strong that, if anything, it was dragging her further down, billowing out her white dress like a jellyfish. The noise of both the swirling water and steam engine nearby filled her ears. As bubbles of air escaped her mouth, Alice was sure she began to see her life flashing before her eyes. As it turned out, it was a flash of silver as two giant minnows shot past her.

It seemed she was destined to drown, become fish food or both, so it was rather peculiar that Alice found herself worrying instead about the red shoes that she had left back on dry land. Her mother had bought them for her the day before as a going away present and she would be cross should Alice lose them so soon. She could hear her mother's voice even now: "You must face the consequences of your actions."

The minnows lost interest in Alice as fast as they had appeared and the cause was soon revealed. A huge curtain of river weed swayed like poplars in the wind, then parted as the head of a hungry perch came into the open water. It glided slowly towards Alice, allowing her just enough time to regret not feeding the fish earlier. *One, two, three, four, five, once I caught a fish alive. Six, seven ...*

Alice was out of breath, literally. With a rush of adrenalin, she found the strength to kick her feet wildly and propel herself a short way towards the sunlight above her. Another two kicks and she bobbed to the surface like a fishing float. She wanted to tread water and catch her breath but she knew the cruel perch was hot on her tail. A quick look around told her she was half way between the riverbank and the train. The problem was that she no longer had the strength to swim to either, let alone outpace a hungry fish.

The solution to her predicament came in the shape of a large white lifebelt, which landed nearby with a slap on the water. She looped it over her head and as she felt herself being reeled in towards the train, two thoughts struck her; *firstly, what would the effect of bait skimming across the surface have on the perch and secondly, what was a lifebelt doing on board a train?*

In no time at all, several pairs of hands pulled her up the side of the carriage and in through an open window. She landed in a wet heap on the floor and a make-shift curtain of coats and blankets rose up around her. A single hand holding a bundle of clothes appeared from behind the curtain and a rather shaky voice belonging to a lady said in a West-Country accent: "Here you go my dear. Change into these dry clothes. They'll be too small for you because they belong to my grand-daughter. But at least you won't catch cold."

"Don't fuss so," said a male voice, "she'll have to learn to stand on her own two feet some time."

This was easier said than done. As Alice shed her wet white dress and put the clothes on, the train rocked from side to side. While she did this, she became aware that the train's whistle was in fact the combined noise of the shrieking passengers. *Thank goodness they've stopped screaming in this carriage*, thought Alice, imagining she would otherwise go quite deaf.

She soon found herself clothed in undergarments and a yellow dress two sizes too small. *Just the type of clothes my mother buys me*, thought Alice, *too small and child-like*. But she had to admit that at least her new clothes were dry and made her feel instantly warmer. She rubbed her hair dry and carefully sipped a cup of hot, sweet tea that had seemed to appear from nowhere. Once she was dressed, the curtain dropped to reveal a very bizarre group of people indeed. They were all very old with distinctive and highly unusual features – bulbous or long noses, large flat or pointed ears, beady or saucer-like eyes, thin or broad faces. Not one of them came even close to being normal. They stood or sat in a circle around Alice.

The carriage they were in, like its travellers, had seen better days. The leather upholstery of the seats was worn and the rugs that covered the old wooden floorboards were fraying at the edges. A musty smell of wood and tobacco filled the air.

"Are you all right my dear?" said the woman who had apparently handed her the clothes. She was an old lady with tight white curly hair and small rimmed glasses, which sat on the end of a long, broad nose. She wore what appeared to be a white sheepskin coat and a little too much jewellery. She reminded Alice of a sheep – one that was trying to look younger than her days. Her voice trembled as she spoke. "That was quite a fall you had."

"We all have falls," barked an old man next to her (the one who had spoken earlier). His large ears, bloodshot eyes and grey moustache that extended into long whiskers made him look like a bloodhound. "Especially at our age. She's young. She'll be fine. Just needs to toughen up a bit."

Alice felt she should speak up. "I'm fine really, all things considered. And thank you very much for rescuing me."

"It was you, who was supposed to rescue us," grunted a rather corpulent man, whose broad face bore some unsightly bumps on his cheeks and jowls. He looked like a wart-hog. "Didn't you hear us shouting 'Daisy Chain!'? You were supposed to make one and use it as a lifeline to pull our train ashore." He shook his enormous head and added a few words under his breath. "Wretched youth!"

"Don't scold her!" said a rather tall, elegant lady with a long neck and large lips. She would have been quite beautiful had it not been for the large liver spots all over her skin. She reminded Alice of a giraffe. "She tried her best. You can't blame *her* for the situation *we* got ourselves into."

Alice looked closely at the other people gathered around her; a small old man of swarthy complexion and red eyes dressed in a black leather coat, who reminded Alice of a fruit bat; a thin lady with smooth shiny skin and the kind of tiny black eyes, nose and mouth that wouldn't have looked out of place on a snake; a short, fat lady with a thin, pointed face and a huge head of bristly hair like a hedgehog's; a positively ancient gentleman whose wrinkly neck and face poked out of his stiff-collared shirt like a tortoise's head; and a rather large old woman, whose huge eyes sat high on her fleshy head, reminding Alice of a toad. Alice sighed inwardly as she did not relish the company of old people. They seldom spoke of anything else but "the good old days". And they often smelled strange.

The momentary silence that ensued allowed Alice to spit out several questions that were teetering precariously on the tip of her tongue. "Please, could you answer me something. Where on earth am I? Who are you all and where are you going? How come this train is so small and what's it doing in the river?"

The hedgehog-lady spoke up. "I'm not sure we can answer all those questions in one answer. In fact, I'm sure we can't. It would take quite a time to construct such a long and complex answer."

"Impossible!" snapped the dog-man. "Can't be done. One at a time. Only way."

Alice recalled someone saying that they could believe six impossible things by breakfast and it was now well past lunch-time. But she remained silent.

"Let me start with who we are," said the giraffe-lady, who seemed to be sipping a dry martini. "My name's Marjory. You'll have noticed that all of us are old. I think that's probably why we are all on this train."

"Except you," mumbled the wart-hog-man, looking at Alice. "You don't belong here."

"The funny thing is, none of us can remember how we got here," said the toad-lady.

"I remember I packed my suitcase for a visit to my daughter's family," said the sheep-lady. "But then...after that ... I can't remember."

"I can remember vivid details from my childhood like it was yesterday," said the hedgehog-lady excitedly. And then began to sob. "But I can't remember yesterday."

"Well if it's any consolation, I can't remember yesterday either," said Alice trying to comfort her.

"And that's why you're here!" said the dog-man with a little too much self-satisfaction. He faced her and bowed. Alice curtsied back. She had never seen a dog bow before, though she'd heard many make that sound. "The name's Pavlov, Colonel Pavlov from K9 division. Name, rank and number is all I need to give. Good job really 'cos it's all I remember."

"Pleased to meet you. But how did your train get in the river?" asked Alice.

"Before we departed, I distinctly heard the train driver talking about wanting to wet his whistle," said the hedgehog-lady. "Could that be of any help?"

"Often is," said Marjory, taking another sip from her glass. "I say, I wonder if this is some kind of cruise?"

Typical of old people, thought Alice. She was getting nowhere fast. "Were you all going on an outing? A day-trip to Brighton perhaps?"

"Why would we be going to Brighton?" asked the bat-man timidly. His glassy red eyes frightened Alice but his voice was rather squeaky and it was all she could do not to giggle.

"Well it does say "Brighton Express" on the outside of the locomotive, you know."

"That doesn't prove anything," boomed the wart-hog man in a deep voice. "I'm wearing a Chesterfield coat but I'm not travelling there." He then frowned and looked thoughtful. "My name's Chester though. Funny that."

13

Everybody suddenly began looking for tags on the insides of their clothing.

"I have an ulster coat," piped up the bat-man. "But I'm not going there. Well, not that I can remember anyway. And my name's not Ulster, it's Kevin."

"But names on coats are not quite the same thing as having the name of a seaside town on the side of a train, you know," said Alice gently, aware that the elderly often took offence at being corrected.

"Are we on our way to Ireland?" inquired the snake-lady. "I'm a little deaf."

"A little slow too," said Chester, the wart-hog man unkindly.

"I heard that," hissed the snake-lady.

Alice decided to change the subject before things became more unpleasant. "Why are you all so small?"

"I beg your pardon! We're the same size as you," croaked the toad-lady in a deep, crackly voice. Speaking made her flesh ripple and Alice was rather glad she was on the opposite side of the carriage.

"I think I can answer that," said the tortoise-man slowly, who until now had remained silent. "You see, I overheard my daughter ... saying to her husband ... 'Jeremiah's a waste of space.'... So if we are now smaller than we were ... we must be taking up far less space. Which is a good thing ... isn't it?"

"Pardon me for saying so," replied Alice, "but that doesn't make too much sense."

"That's exactly what I told my daughter ... because they had a very large house ... you know. I wouldn't have got under their feet. I could have lived ... in the basement. Or even ... under it."

"No, I mean, how can you suddenly shrink when you get old?"

"It's a scientific fact that you get smaller when you age," said the wart-hog-man. "What do they teach children at school these days?"

"I'm not at school any more, I'm going to college," said Alice, instantly realising that this wasn't very relevant to the discussion. "In any case, ageing is a gradual process."

"Tell that to the cabbage white butterfly in the next carriage!" said the snake-lady. The passengers immediately began talking to one another about who should inform the cabbage white.

The hedgehog-lady leaned towards Alice and whispered in her ear. "Let's not do that, she's sleeping."

"Sleeping? At her age?" said the toad-lady. "What a waste of a life!"

Alice was none the wiser and as it had become a heated conversation, she decided to stop asking questions and give the others time to cool off. She glanced out of the dirty windows and saw that they were floating past a huge grey boulder. Half an hour ago, this would have seemed the size of a croquet ball to Alice. Now it was the size of a house. *What a strange dream this is,* she said to herself.

Above the noise of the river and steam engine (the shrieking in the other carriages had thankfully died down),

Alice heard the pitter patter of feet inside the train. The others heard it too and soon everyone stopped talking and looked from side to side to see where the sound was coming from.

All at once, the carriage was full of a loud ringing noise. Alice looked down to see one of the strangest sights she had ever seen. In the middle of the floor was a black telephone. Although it was a relatively new invention, she knew what a telephone was, as she had seen images of one in her father's newspaper. It had been headline news because England, France and America were once again arguing over who had invented it. How clever of them to invent a machine that let people from different countries argue with each other without travelling abroad. Alice was certain that once countries had figured out that they could also talk about nice things with each other over the telephone, there would be no more wars.

But it was not the telephone as such that struck her as strange. It was the fact that it had arms, legs and a face. Two spindly arms protruded from the machine and cradled the receiver, which Alice knew one had to use in order to talk and listen. Two equally thin legs supported the body of the machine. There was a circular face in the middle of the device with numbers and letters that were currently positioned to form a rather angry expression. The telephone's face was bright red and every time it rang, the receiver shook so violently that the machine's arms clearly struggled to hold it in place.

"Someone should answer it!" cried Alice. "Before the poor contraption explodes."

"Do you know how?" asked the hedgehog, for by now the passengers had become more creature than human. "Because I don't."

"Nor me," sighed Jeremiah, the tortoise. "It'll need someone ... a lot smarter than me ... to make it work."

"Well, I am going to college, you know," said Alice, regretting saying it a second time in the space of five minutes. Nevertheless, she had inadvertently volunteered herself and bending down, lifted the receiver from the telephone's hands and held it to her head.

"Huuuuuuah!" is the correct spelling of the noise the telephone made as it exhaled loudly.

"27 seconds!" shouted the telephone. "It took you 27 seconds to answer me. It's simply not good enough! Do you know the number of calls I have to make in a day?"

"I'm sure I don't," replied Alice, apologetically. "I'm very sorry for the delay. But please, could you speak a little more loudly?"

"Try turning the receiver the other way round, Alice," said the telephone smugly and calmed down enough for its face to turn from red to pink. Alice felt rather foolish whereas all the creatures thought she was terribly bright to get even this far.

"Thank you," said Alice. "I have to admit this is the first time I've ever used a telephone."

"That is abundantly clear." The telephone's face had almost reached white but now it returned to a deep pink again. "However, I am not a mere telephone, I am a MOBILE TELEPHONE!" it shouted and added more calmly, "Perhaps you saw the legs?"

"I do apologise. That must make you an extra-special telephone then."

"Yes, it does. You're right, it does." The telephone was clearly pleased with Alice's observation and the pink colour of its face receded to two small dots on its cheeks as it blushed. Alice suspected the telephone had something important to tell them and figured that tact might be the best approach.

"And you knew my name. That was very clever of you too."

Shifting its digits, the telephone frowned. "Not really. I know the names and whereabouts of everyone in Wonderland. That's how I found you. MESSAGE!"

Everyone in the carriage jumped as the telephone screamed out the last word at the top of its voice.

"I knew there was something I had to tell you, Alice. It's a message from the Cheshire Cat. He can't talk to you himself as his phone is engaged. In any case, it's only a fixed phone."

"No legs?" enquired Alice.

"No legs."

The telephone coughed, arranged it digits to look serious and spoke in a very formal manner. "Listen carefully, Alice, for I cannot repeat the Cheshire Cat's message to you again:

Take your time and when you rhyme, pay heed the weir-wolf's measure,

For then a leap comes next.

Follow true advice to you, all the best, from Cheshire

Dial 4 to get this as text."

With that the telephone took the receiver from Alice, folded its legs up underneath itself and to all intents and purposes, went dead.

"How peculiar," exclaimed Alice.

"Very strange," agreed Marjory, the giraffe, who struggled to hold her head upright. "It didn't say goodbye."

"I meant the message. Very peculiar message."

"What does it all mean?" squeaked Kevin the bat and drew his coat tighter round his body in fear.

"The first part was quite clear to me," said Pavlov, the dog. "No rushing. Look before you leap. Think first, then action. Sound advice to me."

"But what's that got to do ... with rhyming?" drawled Jeremiah, the tortoise, sticking his neck out for once and looking more confused than ever.

"I don't like the sound of a werewolf," said the sheep shakily. "Any kind of wolf is too much for me. They sometimes come at you in disguise, you know."

"And a leap?" gulped the toad. "What's all that about? If anyone knows about leaping around here it's me."

"Here are my two cents, for what they are worth," grunted Chester, the warthog. Alice was about to say that two cents would be worth exactly that but after a cold stare from him she thought better of it and closed her mouth. "The words 'measure' and 'Cheshire' rhyme badly. That could be an important clue to understanding the whole message."

I very much doubt it, thought Alice, but held her tongue. She heard the train's whistle, which meant people in the other carriages had begun screaming again. She looked out of the carriage window and saw that they were sailing at quite a speed past a cliff face the size of a castle. She realised there was something else than dirty window panes clouding their view. It was clouds of spray from the river. Not for the first time that day, Alice's tummy took a tumble. Increasing speed, water spray, louder noises and rocks. She put two and two together and came to just one conclusion.

"Listen up everybody. We're heading towards the weir!"

Every now and then, Alice heard the call of a cuckoo or the hollow knocking of a woodpecker, which echoed eerily as if the woods were made up of many rooms. She tried to peek inside the forest but she couldn't see the wood for the trees.

CHAPTER 2

THE WEIR-WOLF

Ordinarily, one could wade through the weir and step down to the lower river without getting one's knees wet, it was that small a drop. Alice had done it several times, much to the disdain of her sisters, who knew their mother hated Alice getting her dress wet. However, being the size she currently was, Alice knew that should she be in the train when it hit a rock or went over the edge, she, along with everyone else on the train, would be crushed to death.

The creatures rushed to windows either side of the train just in time to catch a glimpse of two massive boulders, like gorillas in the mist. As they white-water rafted at the mercy of the river, all they could do was hope that the train kept to the middle of the current and evaded the rocks. A deafening crash towards the rear of the train indicated that a carriage and its unfortunate passengers farther back had not managed to do this.

The train was still picking up speed as another huge boulder loomed up on their left-hand side. Its smooth top was broken by jagged peaks, like the scales or teeth of a dragon.

"Open the windows!" shouted Alice above the roar of the rapids. "Get ready to jump! It's our only chance."

At that, the toad and snake both jumped out of the open window they were sharing. Well, the toad leapt (quite athletically for her bulk) and the snake left in more of a slithery panic.

"Not yet!" shouted Alice but she was too late. The other passengers gazed at the perfect arc the toad jumped in, right up to the point she disappeared into the jaws of a giant salmon. which rose from the water and swallowed her in one gulp. No-one saw the snake but as she was not a water snake, the general feeling was that she didn't make it to dry land. Alice felt especially bad for the snake because she had been hard of hearing and could well have misheard Alice's instructions. She felt partly to blame and vowed to express herself more clearly in future.

"Listen everyone," Alice shouted. "Don't jump until I give the word! And don't take your bags or suitcases with you!" She added this because she knew one was supposed to leave all belongings behind in an emergency.

As Alice repeated the Cheshire Cat's telephone message to herself and tried to make sense of it, she noticed that most of the creatures had returned to their seats. Some had opened their suitcases and were putting on two or even three layers of clothing so as not to leave anything behind. Kevin, the fruit bat, had wrapped a cloak round him over his overcoat, the sheep had emptied her jewellery box over herself and Chester, the wart-hog, had lit up a rather ornate pipe. *Silly old creatures*, thought Alice, *they'll surely drown when they have to swim ashore.* Nevertheless, she picked up a pair of black slip-on plimsolls that had fallen out of someone's bag and put them on. Her bare feet had been getting cold for some time.

"Waste not, want not," said Marjory, the giraffe, who had opened up her lunch box and was handing round ham sandwiches, much to Chester the wart-hog's acute horror. Alice wondered for a moment if the hedgehog felt the same way about ham and if she was in some way related to Chester, as they shared the same surname. The sheep had discovered another flask of tea in her holdall and there was a general clanking of cups and saucers as the animals tried to steady the crockery amidst an increasingly unsteady carriage. Alice wasn't sure whether to admire them for their calmness or yell at them for their stupidity.

She forced her mind back to the telephone message. Patience, rhyming, a werewolf and a leap. *What did it all mean?* And should she also have dialled the number four? She looked outside for inspiration and saw the fuzzy outline of another distant rock formation. Small stones in the river, she mused, yet from here they looked like a herd of elephants. Next, even closer to the train, came a tall thin boulder in the shape of a tower. The creatures gasped at how close they came to hitting it and how fast they skirted round its sharp walls. A loud crack from further back in the train let them know a second carriage had fallen foul of the rapids.

The train suddenly slowed and began to spin round and round as they became trapped in a whirlpool. Some creatures were flung to the floor. Alice knew they couldn't afford to wait much longer before they evacuated.

"We're trapped in an eddy, everyone get ready!" she said.

"It'll suck us down and we're sure to drown," squeaked Kevin.

"Yes or no, is it time to go?" asked Marjory.

"Not yet, but get set."

After a few spins in the eddy, they were catapulted onwards at an even faster pace. They sailed past more rocks, this time taking on the shapes of a large building, the fist of an ogre and a ship.

"We'll be crushed to death!"

"I can't catch my breath," whispered an old nag, who had apparently joined their carriage at some point. She sounded hoarse and the hedgehog kindly rubbed her back as one should do for people who struggle to breathe.

"While we've been floating, I was noting" remarked Alice, "we're talking in rhyme all the time. I don't know how but it can't be long now."

"Take a look across the brook!" shouted Pavlov, the dog. They followed his gaze and saw a large grey rock in the shape of a dog's head. No, not a dog, a wolf. It was the weir wolf the telephone had augured.

When push came to shove, Alice hesitated. *Wouldn't it be easier just to stay in the carriage and take my chances than to jump into the unknown, especially if this is no more than a dream*, she thought. *On the other hand*, she deduced, *if it's a dream then it really doesn't matter either way.* She felt a paw at her back. It was Pavlov, encouraging her to climb through the window. As Alice's courage deserted her, he had taken control.

"Jump! Everyone, jump!" he shouted.

"I'm scared," said Kevin, the fruit bat.

"Everyone has to take a leap of faith at some point in their life," shouted Alice over her shoulder, as she jumped out of the train window and into the cold mist.

The first sensation she had as she entered the white mist was one of cold wetness. When asked later by her sisters whether it was also a wet coldness, she said no, it was quite different. The second thing was that she realised she was falling downwards. It would have been very peculiar had she been falling upwards but given the day's events so far, maybe not out of the question. Thirdly, rather than hit the surface of the water downstream, she continued to fall, and fall. Not only that, but the rate at which she fell seemed to slow with every second. And she also began spinning round in slow motion.

Alice guessed that they had left the rocks behind because bright sunlight now filtered through the spray. Everything was bright white and Alice had to squint her eyes half shut to see anything. Several feet away, Kevin was falling upside down. *He must feel quite at home*, thought Alice. A little farther away were Pavlov and Jeremiah, both looking ill at ease with their descent. Of the other creatures there was no sign.

Far below them, the sun's rays had created a rainbow across the mist. Alice had seen rainbows before but not one quite like this. In addition to the seven colours of the rainbow (Richard Of York Gave Battle In Vain, Alice said to herself as she ticked off the colour against the mnemonic) she counted at least four more, though she was not able to name or describe them. They were totally new colours.

As they fell through the rainbow, the four travellers began to glitter with the colours their clothes and skin came into contact with. Kevin seemed to be very taken with his colourful cloak whereas the now-red-and-blue Pavlov had entered a new level of discomfort. Jeremiah was pleased to get red, yellow and blue on his shell, that was until it mixed up into a dark grey sludge colour. Alice was delighted that she had picked up some of the new colours. She only wished she could have found the words to describe them to her sisters later on.

As they descended, the air became colder and sky clearer. Yet whichever direction Alice looked in, everything was whiter than white and brighter than bright.

"I can see trees down below," barked Pavlov. "Fir trees if I'm not mistaken."

"Nonsense," replied Jeremiah. "How can there be ... a forest in the river?"

"I'm a dog. I think I know a tree when I see one."

Alice could also make out what seemed to be the tree tops of a vast green forest some way below them. In fact, they seemed to be heading for a small clearing in the forest which, apart from the trees, was white like everything else around them.

"How peculiar. I've seen a river in a forest but never the other way round. On the other hand, I've never fallen down a weir before."

"We should name this place, Alice Falls," said Kevin.

"Thank you. That's very thoughtful of you," replied Alice.

They continued to float downwards. The lower they went, the slower they fell. After a while, Jeremiah spoke up: "You know ... I fear we may never reach the ground."

"Don't be ridiculous," snapped Pavlov. "We're bound to reach the ground at some point."

"Not necessarily," joined in Alice, remembering a trick her tutor used to play on her. "If our pace slows continuously by half, we will always cover half the distance left. Therefore, we will continue to get closer to the ground but we will never reach it."

Alice looked across at Kevin, who was shivering with cold or in fright.

"Although in this case," she added quickly, "I'm sure we will."

The group of travellers did indeed reach the ground, albeit at a very slow pace, which was just as well for Alice was upside down at the moment of impact. Based on the crunching sound and coldness against her scalp, Alice figured that they had landed on fresh snow. The water and spray from the river had apparently frozen and fallen to earth as snow. How was it possible that at the top of the weir it was summer and down here it was winter? She had never experienced such a sudden change in the weather.

Alice, Kevin and Pavlov stood up, brushed themselves off and watched as the last of their company – Jeremiah – floated slowly onto his back. He left an unsightly grey stain on the snow where his colours from the rainbow had rubbed off.

"How undignified ... I do apologise!" said Jeremiah, as they turned him over, his legs and arms waving around like a broken windmill.

"Don't mention it," said Alice and wondered if all tortoises were this helpless when on their backs, or whether it was just because he was old.

The group of four took stock of their surroundings. They had indeed come to ground in a small forest glade. The clearing was a perfect circle with four straight paths leading into the surrounding forest. The paths left the clearing in four different directions, in the exact same places as the numbers 3, 6, 9 and 12 on a clock. On closer inspection, Alice noticed that someone had actually drawn those very same numbers on each of the paths. However, unlike a clock, the order of the numbers, starting at the top, went clockwise like this: 6, 9, 12 and 3.

"Not a very clockwise person who drew that," remarked Alice. "How on earth are we supposed to know which is north, east, south and west with the numbers jumbled?"

"Quite so," said Pavlov, "though I believe I have solved the problem. It's quite easy. Safety in numbers."

"How clever of you. Please do tell. Whatever we do, it's important to stay together." Alice was referring to the four of them as she had no idea where the rest of the passengers in her carriage had got to.

"Absolutely," answered Pavlov and bounded off down path number 3 with his tail between his legs, as well he might. He was out of sight before any of the others could make a sound.

"How beastly of him!" said Alice. "And hypocritical. He said himself that we stand a much better chance of survival if we stick together."

"You're so right. I don't know what I'd do if I didn't have you two!" squeaked Kevin in quite a flap. He spread his multi-coloured cloak, fluttered around in a circle twice and then flew off down path number 9 as though he wanted to find out the answer to his own question.

"What's got into those two?" asked Alice. "There was never a wise decision made in rashness. More haste, less speed."

"I know all about that," said Jeremiah slowly. "Have I told you ... about the race I once had ... with a hare?"

"Oh please, not that. I don't think I could bear to hear that story yet again." Her grandmother never failed to tell the story to her whenever Alice commented on how slowly she did things.

"Well, I never ... heard such impudence!" slurred Jeremiah and withdrew his head inside his shell. His voice echoed from inside: "Everyone said ... I should come out of my shell ... more often ... but as soon as I do ... I get my head bitten off."

Alice regretted being so rude to Jeremiah but no amount of apologies could induce him out again. She was at a complete loss as to what to do. She stood and waited. But as there was no-one to offer her any advice and she was getting colder by the minute, she was forced to choose a path on her own. But which path should she

31

choose, number 6 or 12? Or should she follow Colonel Pavlov along path 3 or Kevin down path 9? Pavlov had claimed to have solved the puzzle but she didn't see how.

Working on the odd assumption that 12 was probably north, Alice chose the path behind her. To her delight, once she had turned round and faced number 12, she found it was now at the top of the circle, which felt just like north.

It was only after she had taken a couple of steps forward, she noticed that the number 12 was not in actual fact drawn onto the path. Someone had carefully placed countless pebbles of varying colours and patterns to form the numbers 1 and 2. She bent down to pick up one of the stones. It was smooth, the size of a large marble and mottled liked granite. It was so light that, doubting it was made of stone at all, Alice put the object to her nose and sniffed at it. It had a sweet fragrance. Should she taste it or not? Eventually, Alice licked it. Yes, it was candy. She realised she hadn't eaten in ages. She wondered whether she should take a bite or not. In the end, she couldn't resist a nibble. It tasted of fresh bread so she took another bite. This time it tasted of roast chicken. A third piece - marzipan - finished it off.

She waited a while, for experience told her that the price of tasting any peculiar food was invariably growing larger or shrinking. Nothing happened so she bent down and ate another sweet. This time it was a shiny black pebble that tasted of liquorice, smoked salmon and then cheese. Again, there was no change in her size either way but she did feel guilty that she was ruining the simple but elegant mosaic someone had taken time to create. Her guilt soon vanished as she told herself that anyone using sweets for writing messages was asking for trouble and shouldn't be surprised if someone else came along at some point and gobbled them up. She took three more and put them in the pocket of her dress for later. *Everything has a consequence*, she thought.

Alice looked around. Despite the strange landscape, odd companions and peculiar events of the last hour, there was something familiar about it all. *I've been here before*, she thought to herself. Without a doubt, she knew that she had returned to Wonderland.

After telling Jeremiah which path she was taking and saying that she hoped he would follow her, Alice continued walking along the path. After a few dozen steps, she became painfully aware that her yellow summer dress and black plimsolls were not designed for walking in winter weather. Each crunch her feet made on the snow was followed by a cold, wet feeling as the frosty flakes seeped over the rim of her shoes and melted. In a similar fashion, her dress allowed her to feel the sun on her legs and arms, but also let the icy air in. Was everything here a mixture of extreme enjoyment and acute discomfort? Alice began to think there was something to be said for moderation.

The snow-covered path ran ahead of Alice until it reached the distant blue horizon. On either side stood the tall dark green walls of the forest. Everything shrank in straight lines as it converged on the vanishing point, which could have been ten miles or a hundred miles away. Alice pressed on.

Every now and then, Alice heard the call of a cuckoo or the hollow knocking of a woodpecker, which echoed eerily as if the woods were made up of many rooms. She tried to peek inside the forest but she couldn't see the wood for the trees.

She considered venturing into the woods to see if the going under foot was warmer and drier but a voice in her head (oddly reminiscent of her father's) told her that one should never stray from the straight and narrow, especially in strange places. She hoped the voice was from her memory as opposed to a real voice. This was not a good time or place to go mad. Quite so, agreed the voice.

Alice ignored the voice in her head, left the path and stepped into the woods. The fir trees grew close together like a pack of cards. Their branches intertwined as if they were holding hands to bar Alice's way. Despite the fact that the foliage had kept most of the snow out, it was still bitterly cold. And dark.

Alice wasn't wearing a red hooded cloak. Nevertheless, she decided to pick up a small branch from the forest floor. *I may not be able to fight off a wolf with this*, she thought, *but it might run after it if I throw it and shout 'Fetch!'*

This was not a beautiful forest in the fairy tale sense and Alice would have returned to the path had it not been for the unexpected sight of a white door wedged between two fir trees. *How bizarre to find a door in a forest*, she thought. Alice walked round to the other side of the door to see what was there. It was as she had expected, the other side of the door.

As good manners were instilled in Alice, as they were in most young people of that time, she knocked on the door, supposing that if there were anyone not wishing her to open it, they would say so. No sound came from within, so she entered.

Beyond the open door was a small square room all in white, with a white door in the middle of each wall. *I was right*, thought Alice, (in a way that wrongly suggested she was right most of the time), *the forest is made up of rooms.*

As the air was warmer and the floor drier inside than outside, and because Alice was curious to a fault, she closed the door behind her and waited. *After all, she mused, this does look like a waiting room, and if it's a waiting room, those doors must lead somewhere.* After a minute or two, she became impatient and knocked on each of the other three doors, opening them in turn when no-one answered. Each door led to another room identical to the first one.

"If I'm not careful, I shall get lost," said Alice out loud. She considered this enigma carefully. "If I always take the door on the right-hand wall, then surely I shall arrive back in the place I started from after three rooms. Or is it after four rooms? Just to be sure, I'll leave this twig on the floor, so that I know when I have arrived back in this room. Thank goodness I read Hansel and Gretel."

Alice felt braver now that she had listened to her own voice. She left the room by the door in the right-hand wall. She did the same thing in the next room. And the next. When the room after that didn't have a stick on the floor, she began to get scared. She opened the other doors in the room, saw that they too led to identical rooms and promptly closed them again. *Don't panic*, she thought. *Even if this isn't a dream, I can simply retrace my steps by taking the doors on the left-hand wall.* The trouble was, Alice was no longer sure by which door she had entered.

She guessed and took the next four doors on her left, but none of the rooms had a twig in it. She then decided to go straight ahead through each door for six rooms on the basis that the rooms must lead somewhere. They did. To her dismay, they led to a seventh white room. "I'm truly lost," she said, and tears came to her eyes.

She was startled by a sudden knock on the door to her right. *If it's someone who means to harm me*, she thought, *I'd better remain quiet.* There was another rap on the door. *On the other hand, I am in dire need of help.*

"Come in!" said Alice. But what if she was inviting a wolf into the room, a wolf which understood English and had no manners whatsoever? She would be safer if she were more specific. "But only if you're a friend!"

The door opened and there stood a dark-skinned boy of about her own age. At least, she thought he was a boy as both the facial features and body were rather androgynous. The dark face had unusually high cheekbones and a strong chin and nose, making he or she undeniably handsome. Apart from the face, the rest of the head, arms, legs and the whole of the body were covered in shiny black feathers.

"Hello, I'm Alice," said Alice, standing up and offering her hand.

"I'm a jackdaw.

"Hello Jack."

"Sorry?"

"You said your name was Jack Door."

"No. I said I *am* a jackdaw. And you're an Alice?"

"No. My name is Alice. I'm a girl. A human being." She wondered if this sounded rude to the boy as he did indeed have the same number of legs, arms, eyes and so on as she did. It was just that he was covered in feathers (by now, Alice had decided to call him a boy).

"What's your name?" she asked.

"I don't have one."

"How awful!"

"Why?"

"Well, how do you tell which Christmas presents are yours?"

"What's Christmas?"

Alice had never had a conversation with anyone who didn't know what Christmas was. She wasn't sure if it was possible but she was keen to try.

"You seem lost," said the jackdaw.

"I am. In more ways than one. But how do you know that? Have you been spying on me?" asked Alice.

"Sort of. My job is to look after the doors here – check the handles, oil the hinges, write poems, that sort of thing. There's not much goes on here that I don't know about."

Alice had never met a boy who wrote poetry before. Or one who serviced doors, for that matter.

"Did you pick a twig up off the floor?" she asked.

"What's a twig?"

Alice realised this was not going to be an easy conversation. "Jack Door," she murmured very quietly to herself as she contemplated what to say next.

"Sorry?" said the jackdaw, who seemed to have an extraordinarily good sense of hearing.

"May I call you Jack?" asked Alice.

"If you like. Actually, it would be nice to have a name. Thanks."

Jack smiled and a hundred butterflies came alive in Alice's tummy.

"Excuse me for saying so," said Alice, "but where I come from, jackdaws are birds."

"What are birds?"

"They're creatures covered in feathers." Alice noticed the blank look on Jack's face. "And they can fly."

"Oh, I can't fly. At least, I don't think I can."

Jack flapped his arms up and down. It looked so funny that Alice began to laugh and that made Jack laugh too.

"Somebody like you came here once," said Jack, "and told me that I looked like a jackdaw, so I assumed I'm a jackdaw."

"Do you live in the forest?" asked Alice.

"What's a forest?"

"We're in the forest. These rooms are in the forest."

"Are they? You see, I've never been outside these rooms. At least, I can't remember having been anywhere else."

"What about your family? Or friends? Where are they?"

"I don't think I have any. At least, I haven't seen any creatures that look like me. I've met a few creatures that look like you, and then a few that don't, but it's not often someone finds their way in here. I like helping them find their way back. It's nice to make people happy, isn't it?"

Alice decided that she liked Jack.

"Where do you come from?" he asked.

Alice wasn't sure how to describe another world if Jack was struggling with the basic words of his own one. "I came from the river. Running water." She made a motion with her hand.

"Yes, I know what a river is," said Jack.

"Oh sorry. I came with a group of other people but we got separated. They were very old. I'm a bit worried about them."

"I wouldn't worry too much. A creaking door lasts the longest. I find that old things do just fine with a bit of care."

Alice was sure Jack couldn't have been in the forest rooms all his life.

"Can you remember anything about how you got here?"

"No. I used to think about it but it made me sad. Now I try to keep busy every moment of the day and I'm much happier."

"Is there enough here to keep you busy?"

"Oh yes. At the moment, I'm having trouble with door hinges and rhyming couplets."

Alice burst out laughing then saw she had to explain herself. "I'm sorry, Jack. It's just that I never thought of doors and poems as having much in common with each other."

"Really? They're actually quite similar. If they don't fit perfectly, there's not much you can do with them. And if either are closed to you, then you'll never see what's on the other side."

Alice couldn't help thinking that from what she'd seen, all the rooms were identical and there was nothing new to see. But she didn't want to hurt Jack's feelings.

"Would you recite one of your poems for me?"

"If you like. But I warn you, they may not make much sense."

"Why?"

"Well, I have no idea what most of the words I use mean. And sometimes I change words just because they rhyme better."

"Right. I can see how that might be a problem. Nevertheless, I'd love to hear one."

"Very well." Jack stared at the door on the other side of the room for inspiration. "Here goes."

"I went to a world where frogs could fly, and eels could stand on their heads.

Where daffodils could never die, and buds overslept in their beds.

I climbed a hill of strawberry jam and encountered a man with a key.

He opened a door from the inside out and this he said to me.

'Look after the young, take care of the old, lend beasts a helping hand.

For those are the creatures, despite their worth, you most misunderstand.

*Remember that the camel's humps are not full up with
water.*

*It matters not the lumps it has, it's fat, you see, that's
caught there.'"*

Jack hesitated. "I'm not too keen on that rhyming
couplet. It squeaks a bit and needs adjusting."

"Oh, never mind. It's lovely. Please go on," said Alice,
who was enjoying herself tremendously.

*"Flamingos eat a lot of shrimps but algae make them
pink.*

Dolphins may get thirsty but, you see, they never drink.

Moths are not enticed by flames, it's light they journey to.

Neither do they eat your clothes, their caterpillars do.

*Owls make funny noises but not one will say 'tu-whit
tu-woo'.*

Tiger's live in cages, there's more than in the wild.'"

Alice raised her eyebrows?

"Is that last line bad?" asked Jack.

"It's perfect!" said Alice. "Carry on."

*"Bulls don't see the colour red, they're wholly colour blind
instead.*

*Polar bears aren't left-handed as polar cap explorers
said.*

No ostrich ever put its head inside a sandy floor.

The memory of a goldfish is three months, maybe more.

*Lemmings may get sad sometimes but suicide is not their
goal.*

*Dodos died because of all the forests that the humans
stole.*

Save the children, save the old, but save the creatures first.

Within their grasp our future holds and yet we treat them worst.'

That's all, I'm afraid."

Alice clapped and gazed at Jack. She especially loved the way he made her feel like the poem was meant just for her.

"Where did you get that poem from? Was it really your own?"

"I got it from you, Alice. I just thought of you and the words just came. I've no idea what they meant."

Alice could hardly believe her ears. "You're very special, Jack."

"You too. Meeting another creature is always a special moment for me."

Alice couldn't help thinking that Jack might be under a spell. Perhaps a witch had taken away his memory and coated him in feathers. It would explain why he couldn't remember anything and why he was shut up in these rooms. It didn't explain why, despite his isolation, he seemed so kind and positive about everything.

"Don't you ever get lonely?" she asked.

"What's 'lonely'?" Jack had talked so seldom to other creatures that he had forgotten what many common words meant.

"Lonely means being sad because you're on your own. Don't you want to have someone to talk to, be with?"

"Sometimes. I would be very glad if you would stay with me. I haven't said that to any other creature I've met."

Alice felt the blood rush to her cheeks and she looked away so he wouldn't see.

"Can you stay?"

"That might be a bit difficult. First of all, I don't know you very well. And secondly, my family is probably already wondering where I've got to." *On the other hand*, thought Alice, *this is probably just a dream and I am rather enjoying Jack's company.* "I can stay a while, I suppose."

She turned to look at Jack but he was already busy testing one of the door handles.

"That's OK," he said. "I can show the way out of the rooms, if that's what you want."

"Leave or stay. You make it sound very black and white," she said, not unaware of the stark contrast between his dark feathers and the white of the rooms.

"A door is either open or closed," he replied.

Alice had never met anyone quite like Jack Door. He was clearly quite naïve about people and knew little of the world outside. Nevertheless, he had a confidence and directness that appealed to her. She wouldn't have minded at all if it had taken Jack a little longer to find the way out. As it was, a couple of right-hand doors and a left-hand door later, they were standing in the room with the twig on the floor.

"Here we are," said Jack, "safe and sound. It's that door over there. Is there anything else I can do to make you happy?"

Alice didn't know quite what to say. She smiled at Jack.

"No," she said in rather a strained voice. "But I wish there was something I could to do to repay your kindness. And that lovely poem."

"It's enough to see the expression on your face. You have a beautiful smile."

Once again, Jack left Alice speechless. And breathless. But not motionless. Refusing to follow the rational voice inside her head, Alice walked up to Jack and kissed him lightly. Was she expecting him to shed his feathers and turn into a handsome prince? Or was this just a new way of showing her feelings?

"That was nice. What was it?" asked Jack.

"A kiss," said Alice, feeling the blood rise to her cheeks again as she retreated a couple of steps.

"Could I have another?" said Jack with a smile on his face.

"No," said Alice, trying hard to sound angry but not succeeding very well.

Jack walked up to Alice. She could hear the sound of her heart beating in her ears. Jack held out his hand and presented her with a single shiny black feather.

"It fell out as you gave me that kiss. From here," he said, pointing to his chest, or his heart, depending on whether one was into anatomy or romance.

Alice took the feather slowly and put it in her dress pocket with the three sweets. "Thank you."

"It's nothing," replied Jack, just as Alice was about to say it was the loveliest present she had ever received.

"Jack?"

"Yes?"

"Why don't you come with me instead of staying here on your own?" She said it as nonchalantly as she could make it sound.

There was a short silence as Jack considered her invitation.

"I don't think I can," he replied. "I mean, I want to. But ..." For a moment, Jack's eyes widened as if he remembered something terrifying about his past, beyond the safety of his doors. Then the moment was lost.

"I'd better go," Alice blurted out, confused and embarrassed by everything that had just happened.

"Of course."

Alice turned slowly and tried to turn the doorknob. It wouldn't budge.

"Bit of oil, that's all," said Jack.

Jack's hand brushed against Alice's as he opened the door for her and a rush of cold air met them both. Jack looked out into the woods as if he had never seen them before.

"So those are trees."

"Yes. Woods are beautiful. Or some can be. Come outside with me for a moment. You don't need to be afraid. I'll be right next to you."

Jack hesitated so Alice took his hand. Together they crossed the threshold and stood with the forest before them and the open door at their backs.

Jack smiled. "I don't believe anyone else could have got me to do this, Alice."

Alice gave an involuntary shiver against the winter cold. Jack noticed, opened his arms and folded her in a feathered embrace. Alice felt warm but also safe and whatever the opposite of 'very lonely' was. *I could get used to this*, she thought. She felt Jack shiver.

"Are you cold, Jack?"

He didn't answer. She wondered if he was being brave. But when she looked up into his face, she saw the sweat on his brow. His eyes were bloodshot and his jaw was trembling.

"I can't leave the rooms, Alice. I'm sorry."

He stepped back inside the room and his fever subsided immediately.

"You go, Alice. I'll be fine. I'm sorry."

There was nothing she could say to ease his pain or hers. So she faced the way back to the path and took a few steps.

"Alice?"

She spun round.

"Please don't forget me," he begged.

"Don't worry, Jack, I won't. I'll come back for you, you know. I'll find a way to get you out."

On her way to the path, she looked back once more but the door was shut and Jack Door had gone. She wept more than she had wept for years and the most infuriating thing was, she didn't know why.

Time passed unnoticed and the forest scenery remained much the same. The cold snow nipped at Alice's toes and now and then hidden twigs would scratch her skin. *How can this be a dream*, wondered Alice, *if I can feel the cold and pain? If I can see, hear and smell?*

Alice thought of Jack Door constantly; she relived his every gesture and word to ponder what they may have meant or not meant. It was truly strange that his poem told of animals and how people misunderstood them when she had just met a whole group of them on a train. *What had happened to them*, she asked herself. She felt responsible for them. After all, it was her idea to jump from the train.

From time to time, she also thought of her family, especially her mother and father who, by now, must be worried sick about where she had got to. She had to return home before dark as she still hadn't packed her suitcase.

Most of her thoughts though were of Jack. She tried to think of ways to release him from his prison. But she couldn't think straight. There didn't seem to be enough time to deal with all the thoughts in her head.

Now and again, she took the black feather out of her pocket and held it to her lips. This was normally followed by a smile or a tear or sometimes both. The more distance she put between herself and Jack Door, the sadder she became. It felt as though something had changed within her and she would never be quite the same ever again.

Little by little, thanks to the weak warmth of the sun, the cold white carpet of snow beneath her thinned then vanished altogether, replaced by cold grey slush and then thick dark mud. It somehow reflected Alice's mood. Her legs became caked in grime and her feet wore clay clogs. Her pace slowed as her feet sank into the mire with each step and reappeared lifting their own weight in mud.

"I wish they didn't feel so icy cold," she said out loud, then regretted saying so after she began to lose the feeling in her legs altogether.

Whether it was the effect of the cold or her need for comfort, as she repeated the conversations and moments she had had with Jack over and over in her mind, she unintentionally changed or shortened parts of them each time. What Alice didn't realise, however, was that it was these very memories that gave her the strength to carry on.

Eventually, step by step, mile by mile, the ground began to dry out and harden. She regained the blood circulation in her legs just as she made out a point on the horizon where the Winter Forest seemed to come to an end. Sure enough, a mile or so farther on, she could plainly see where forest gave way to open plain, and where the path carried on into what she hoped would be a more hospitable land. From the depths of her mind a familiar voice sighed and said: "Out of the frying pan and into the fire."

A fetid odour wafted across the land. Alice hoped it was nothing more sinister than an escape of sulphur gas from the swamp. What a shame it wasn't one of the noble gases, she thought. They wouldn't dream of smelling so bad.

CHAPTER 3

MOOR IS LESS

It was all Alice could do not to cry. Unlike the forest, there were no birds here. Possibly no living creatures at all. And no shelter. The land before her stretched flat in all directions until it was lost in the mist. She had entered a brown wasteland of bog, small rocks and dead grass, dotted with puddles or ponds of dirty water. A fetid odour wafted across the land. Something unclean, inhospitable. It was though the land were rotting or sick. Alice hoped it was nothing more sinister than an escape of sulphur gas from the swamp. *What a shame it wasn't one of the noble gases*, thought Alice. *They wouldn't dream of smelling so bad*.

Looking out over the desolate landscape, Alice couldn't help sighing in despair. She wished Jack Door had come with her to keep her company. Or one of her travelling companions from the train. Even the grumblings of Chester, the wart-hog, would be welcome. Any voice but the one originating from her own mind.

With the Winter Forest at her back, Alice set off into the moor. By her reckoning, the sun should have set by now and night should have been upon the land. This was Wonderland, however, where normal rules didn't apply. Although the wasteland was gloomy and a dense mist obscured the sky, she could still make out the vague glow of the sun trying in vain to break through. How much time had really passed? What time was it back home? Did she still have time to pack and catch her train to London or would she end up staying with her parents?

"Be thankful for small mercies" was a phrase Alice's parents used quite often when other people complained about their jobs, the economy, about their husbands or wives, about anything really. At least people had work, they would say. At least they were married. At least they didn't have kids. It was a phrase she couldn't help repeating in her current predicament. At least she had some visibility, a dry path and warmth in the air, she told herself. At least it wasn't wet or cold anymore. Alice disliked how her parents nagged her to look on the bright side of everything. She wasn't even able to be sad and depressed without feeling guilty.

Alice thrust her hand into her dress pocket and moved the three sweets and feather between her fingers. For a moment she wondered why she had a feather with her. When she remembered, her heart sank at the memory of having to leave Jack Door behind. Was she right to leave him?

The path was slightly higher than the land either side, which meant that the waters of the marshland didn't encroach on her trail. This was fortunate, as the pools looked as thick and dark as oil, blood even. There were dozens perhaps hundreds of puddles and ponds on either side of the path. None of them were larger than a school playground but they looked deep, as if they could play home to unspeakable things. More than once, Alice thought she saw ripples on the surface of a nearby pond and hastened on.

As the ground was solid, Alice covered far more of it than when she had trudged through the forest snow. The gloom and disease that afflicted the land, however, remained unchanged.

At one point, off to her left in the distance, she saw tall, thin black creatures, which used long, spindly legs and arms to wade through the waters and catch snake-like fish. Their elongated fingers ended in cruel barbs, which made sure the eels, once caught, could not escape. She hid behind a rock and watched them pass. The name of the Underground station Ealing sprang to mind and, shuddering at the thought these creatures might inhabit the sewers of London, she named the creatures Eelers.

Jack Door would of have protected her, of that she was sure. Her heart sank again when she realised she could no longer conjure up the image of his face in her mind's eye. She began to wonder where she was trying to get to and what the hurry was. She couldn't seem to concentrate on anything else except the fetid air and heaviness in her soul.

On she went, deeper into the mud flats. Her legs were aching, her stomach made noises and she badly needed a bath. She had never been this tired or hungry or dirty before. This was new territory for her in more ways than one. Her step had slowed to a snail's pace as she had no reason to make an effort. She didn't even know why she had been hiding from the Eelers. Intuitively, seeking some kind of comfort, her fingers touched the feather in her pocket. She could not recall how it had got there but she felt its softness, warmth and power. It was the only thing left that mattered to her. There was something about it that forced her to put one foot in front of another. To keep going.

Initially as just an inkling, then a certainty, Alice detected a slight breeze in the air, blowing from the direction she was walking in. It was warm and carried more of the same rank odour of the marshland. At least she wasn't cold ... she stopped herself from completing the sentence, but she didn't know why.

The warm breeze grew in strength and the mist began to clear. As the land revealed itself, it gave Alice no reason for hope. The marshland simply duplicated itself as far as the eye could see. The colourless landscape merged into a sky of dull grey with no horizon. This was no sky of menacing storm clouds, no drama here, but an impossibly vast dome of sullen grey, as forsaken as the land beneath it.

Another group of Eelers strode slowly along in the distance, their black nets bulging with pond life. Alice stood still but didn't bother to hide. Once they were out of sight, she continued, with the feather cradled in her hand.

Gradually, the breeze grew into a wind, warm and humid, then into gusts, fierce enough to throw dust into Alice's eyes. Its ghostly howl moaned across the moor. Alice hoped it was the wind and not the calls of creatures rising from the dark pools, though she didn't know why. She bent her head and shielded her eyes to make sure she could see well enough to stay on the path. A few paces on, Alice found herself having to push with her legs and body against what was now a gale, in order to make progress. Grit blasted her arms and legs like a thousand wasp stings. The moaning had risen to a howl, making it even more like the cries of a crazed beast. Out of the corner of her eye, Alice spied a group of rocks. Drawing on the stamina and resolve that the feather seemed to give her, she decided that she needed to get out of this sandstorm and take shelter for a while.

Against her better judgment, she stepped off the path towards an outcrop of rocks, perilously close to a dark pool. In the same instant, the wind vanished as though it had never been there. All was still and tranquil. The air was still rank and warm, and the marshland spread out around her in every direction. But the wind had gone. She looked back to the path, which appeared peaceful and untroubled by the storm she had encountered not a minute before. However, when Alice extended her arm across the edge of the path, she again felt the full force of the wind and the countless pin-pricks of grit against her skin.

She was so mystified by the phenomenon that at first, she didn't notice a faint ringing sound. Once she did, the noise instantly reminded her of a telephone on a train, and how angry it had been at not being answered right away. *How strange*, she thought, *I'd forgotten all about the river, the train and that telephone.* Alice searched feverishly among the rocks to find out where the ringing was coming from. Sure enough, wedged in a crevice between two large stones was a black telephone, holding the receiver in its hands, pink in the face and not looking at all happy.

Alice quickly bent down and lifted the receiver, making sure she held it the right way round this time. The telephone spoke up, its face slowly returned to the normal white:

"Much better. You answered faster this time. However, you've no idea how long I've been following this path, ringing my hands and waiting for you to answer."

"I'm awfully sorry. But I had no idea you were there. Why didn't you step onto the path and let me know?"

"With all that wind? You wouldn't have heard or seen me. In any case, whoever heard of someone answering a telephone in the middle of the road! That's dangerous. Don't be ridiculous."

"Whoever heard of a telephone in a train on a river!" retorted Alice and faced the other way.

"My, you do have a temper. I should say at this point that I'm a different telephone to the one you met on the river."

Alice turned around. "But you look exactly the same."

Judging by the sudden redness of the telephone's face, Alice realised she had offended it. Perhaps she had been a little tactless. *After all, don't all kettles look the same? Bicycles too. Tigers, bananas and safety pins for that matter. The list is endless. Why, perhaps the telephone thinks all people look the same, with two eyes, one nose and one mouth always in the same place.*

"I do apologise," said Alice, suspecting that she had been doing rather a lot of this since arriving in Wonderland, "but if you aren't the same telephone, how do you know about my exchange with the other one?"

The telephone calmed down and rearranged its digits into a smug expression.

"I'm rather well connected. Especially when it comes to exchanges."

"I am truly sorry that you've had to walk so far," said Alice after a short pause.

"Not to worry, it's a long-distance call anyway." The telephone turned its feet inward so Alice could catch a glimpse of its running shoes.

Alice remembered the telephone message that she had received on the train. "Do you have another message for me from the Cheshire Cat?" she asked.

"Better than that. I have a call waiting from him. Please hold."

There was a whir and a click and the digits on the telephone's face moved to appear as though the telephone were closing its eyes.

"Hello, Alice? Is that you?" The voice on the other end sounded vaguely familiar.

"Yes, is that you?"

"Who?"

"The Cheshire Cat?"

"Yes, it's me. Thank goodness. For a moment I thought you were going to tell me I was someone else. As you may remember, I'm rarely my whole self at the best of times. At worst, in theory, I could become somebody totally different."

Alice didn't know what to say to this and suspected that anything further she might say would only lead to more confusion. So she kept quiet.

"Can we start again?" asked the Cheshire Cat at length. "How are you doing, Alice?"

"Not very well, I'm afraid." At that she burst into tears. She tried to relate recent events but she had difficulty in recalling much at all. She remembered the river and the train and something about animals but that was about it. She was overwhelmed and now suddenly having someone to talk to was simply too much. She sobbed as she struggled to describe the Winter Forest.

"I'm sorry it's been so tough for you," said the Cheshire Cat. "I wish I were there to help you in person, so to say. Even a part of me. Unfortunately, I'm somewhere else."

"Where are you exactly?"

"I haven't the foggiest. It's quite dark in here and cramped and smells of cupboards. I'd send you a photograph but it's too dim to develop one let alone take one."

"So you can't see anything but darkness?"

"I can't even see that. Though I know it's here and it's stopping me see other things."

"It sounds a bit scary. I'm being rather selfish talking about my troubles all the time when you appear to have enough of your own."

"Poppycock. A trouble shared is a trouble halved. Now we've shared our troubles, we have ... erm..."

"The same number of troubles we started with?"

"Ah yes, I knew there was a catch somewhere. The point is, I telephoned you to tell you that things are going to get better from now on. I figured that coming back to Wonderland might be disorientating for you. I'm sure you're wondering why everything's so different from last time; the creatures, the places, even the weather."

"But that's just it. I can't remember much about anything. Not even how I got here."

"Oh. Do you remember your parents and home? Dinah, your cat? Going to college?"

Blurred images of home drifted across Alice's mind as though it were itself a wilderness. As if from a distant half-forgotten dream. Something wasn't right at home. Alice realised she had to get back there.

"Now you're in Wonderland. You came down the waterfall," said the Cheshire Cat.

"But why am I here?"

"My guess is that we need you. Things have been getting steadily worse here. That's probably why you've returned to us!"

"But what am I supposed to do here?

"I'm not sure. What do you want to do? Everyone needs a purpose in life. Or was it a porpoise?"

Alice carefully considered her answer. "Right now, I think I want to get back home, wherever that is."

"Well, that sounds a splendid place to start. Why don't you start from there?"

"How can I start from home if I can't get back there in the first place? I can't even remember what it looks like."

"I mean why don't you start with that goal – to reach home?"

"Oh I see." The Cheshire Cat's advice made sense. "That's a good idea, yes. Thank you. I have a goal. But I still don't know where to start."

"Let me think. Well, if I were you, if one wants to go *back* somewhere, one should retrace one's steps from whence one came. That would seem the shortest way back, don't you agree?"

It made some odd kind of sense but Alice also sensed there was a flaw to the Cheshire Cat's thinking. If she wasn't mistaken, there usually was. She had now remembered enough about the wasteland and the cold forest to know that she couldn't face going that way back. And if there was a waterfall, how could she scale it without wings? She told the Cheshire Cat as much.

"In that case, you only have one alternative but to go forwards. They say that the longest way round is the shortest way home."

"I'm not getting back onto that path again. No way! I shall die!" sobbed Alice.

"Why do you need to you return to the path? Why not walk beside the path where it's warm and dry and there's no wind?"

"Can I do that?"

The silence on the other end said plenty. It said, for a college student, you are not very bright. It begged the question, why do you not think for yourself?

"What do your senses tell you, Alice?" said the Cheshire Cat, breaking the silence.

"Which one? I have five, you know; sight, hearing, taste, smell and touch."

"You have a good many more than that, you know. How about your sense of balance, or sense of distance? Or sense of meaning or decorum? Or sense of danger? You'll need to start using all your senses to survive in Wonderland. Courage now, Alice. Head for the Halfway House. It's not far away. And please call me Cheshire. Most of my friends do and we are, after all, very old friends.

"Just one thing before you go. I suspect something dark has come to Wonderland. I think it may have locked me in this wardrobe. It's bringing about dreadful changes; extreme weather conditions, a sickness in the land, unkind behaviour in the people. I suspect that finding your way back home has something to do with helping us rid Wonderland of this malevolence. Good luck, Alice. And be careful. I have to go now and try to open this cupboard door. As long as it's not locked, I should be out in no time. Let's talk again soon."

There was a loud click on the line.

"That's it," said the telephone. "He's gone."

"I see. Well, thank you again for making it possible for me to talk to him."

"It's funny," said the telephone, "we machines would have the capability to revolutionise your lives, but here we are passing mundane messages back and forth. Imagine if everyone had a telephone. People wouldn't need to think for themselves."

"Which would not be a good thing," said Alice.

With that, the telephone shuddered and went dead.

Alice didn't have as much time to digest the Cheshire Cat's words as she would have liked because she noticed a small package lying next to the telephone. It hadn't been there before the call. It was cube-shaped, wrapped in greaseproof paper and held together with a blue ribbon tied up in a bow. On the side, it said "EAT ME". She opened the gift (any package tied up so prettily was sure to be a present) and found four rounds of cheese and pickle sandwiches. Despite the puzzle as to how the package had appeared, she was sure it was from Cheshire and posed no danger. And she was very hungry. Perhaps if he was able to send advice and best wishes over the telephone, he could also send her sandwiches. Applying a little of Cheshire's own brand of logic, Alice found herself dwelling less on the question of how the food parcel had arrived and whether it was safe to eat or not, and more on the question of why her benefactor had opted to send her Cheddar cheese as opposed to Cheshire.

Encouraged by the Cheshire Cat's words and his food for thought, Alice began walking alongside the path and eating at the same time. The sandwiches were delicious. She walked close to the path and made sure she stayed well away from the dark pools.

Her spirits rose further when not too far ahead in the distance, she saw what looked like a cottage. She judged that it would take about half an hour at a swift walking pace to get to there. She hadn't seen the house earlier but that was not surprising since visibility in the storm had been poor and she hadn't been able to see more than two feet in front of her. Now, with her destination in sight, no wind, a weak but nevertheless warm sun seeping through the mist and food in her stomach, Alice felt happier than she had for a long time. She still didn't have all her memory back but she knew that she had to keep going forward. The feather had helped her through the worst part.

Half an hour later, the cottage seemed no nearer. The moor evidently created optical illusions by making things appear closer than they really were. An hour went by and Alice was relieved to make out more details in the house. It was a simple one-storey white cottage with two windows and a door on the front wall. A wisp of grey smoke rose into the air from a brick chimney.

After another hour, Alice was literally a stone's throw away, not that she would toss a stone at a house, whether it were made of glass or not. She could now see that the roof was thatched and the walls whitewashed. A higgledy-piggledy white wooden fence ran round the house. It would have been an idyllic scene if it weren't for the fact that the windows and door of the house were just holes in the wall. Looking again at the doorway, Alice saw what appeared to be a young girl standing there. The girl waved and Alice waved back as, after all, this was the first real human being she had seen since she had arrived in Wonderland. Alice was relieved to find that she could now remember most things about her family and home, the animals she had met on the train and events in Wonderland. Unknown to her, what she hadn't recalled was anything to do with Jack Door.

It took Alice ten times longer than it should have done to cover just half the distance to the house. She was very frustrated and a little scared as something unnatural was at work.

"More unnatural than being shrunk to the size of an insect and sharing a train carriage with talking beasts?" said Alice out loud to make her argument more convincing. When put like that it did sound very convincing but didn't do much to allay her fears. After what seemed an eternity, Alice arrived at the picket fence.

"Hello!" cried the girl. She was slightly younger than Alice with long black hair full of large curls. Red ribbons held it back from a round pretty face with rosy cheeks. A black bodice covered a white blouse, below which white petticoats billowed out like a waterfall. White ankle socks and shiny red shoes completed the uncanny picture that this girl had just stepped out of one of Alice's old fairy tale books.

"Hello, I'm Mary," she shouted again.

"Hello. I'm Alice. You won't believe how relieved I am to see you!"

"Likewise. Come to the house. But take your time. Getting here may not go as fast as you'd like. We can talk on the way."

It was a strange thing to say given that the two girls appeared to be no more than two dozen paces apart. But she was right about how long it took to cross the small garden. No matter how many or how large steps Alice took over the crazy paving, she covered no more ground than a snail would. Putting in an extra effort to go faster only succeeded in making Alice tired and cross.

"What on earth is this place?" asked Alice, her frustration clearly bubbling to the surface.

"Halfway House. It's half way between the forest and the town."

Alice perked up at the word "town". A town near here? Civilisation? *Thank heavens for small merc* ... thought Alice, and cut herself short before she began to sound just like her mother.

"What's happening when I walk towards you? Why can't I get closer to you?"

"That's to do with the house. It's the same for everyone. They say it's never easy to reach Halfway House. But once you're here, things get easier."

"Do you live here?" Alice wondered how anyone could. *Why, it would take all day to walk anywhere and by the time you got there, it would be time for bed.*

"No," laughed Mary, "I don't live here. But I come here occasionally to tend to the garden."

Alice had had plenty of time to take in the surrounding garden. It was decorated not with flowers, at least not ones which were growing, but with beautifully laid out shells and other objects in tidy rows. Spread out on top of the muddy earth were bells of silver, sea shells and cut flower heads. To Alice, it made perfect sense to create a garden with things that didn't need watering or weeding.

"It's an exquisite garden," said Alice.

"Thank you. I knew you'd like it. The townsfolk say it used to be even more beautiful before. Many years ago, it used to have real nut trees and fruit trees. Legend says that the trees bore fruit made of precious jewels and metals. They say a Spanish princess came to see the garden and coveted the fruit. The owner of the garden – Mr Shafto - a simple but kind man, fell in love with the princess and gave her a silver nutmeg and a golden pear. When she returned to Spain – all princesses return to their castles at some point - she left him broken-hearted and both he and his trees never recovered."

"What a sad story. Does Mr Shafto live here still?"

"No. They say he sailed overseas in search of his princess while his garden withered away. Apparently, she had already married someone else. In my opinion, the princess was terribly mean and the man was daft in the head. I hate them both for what they did to this garden."

Alice was taken aback at the harshness of Mary's comment. "So what happened then?"

"It's a mystery. You know what they say, three may keep a secret if two of them are dead. I hope they withered and died too."

There was clearly no love lost between Mary and the owner of the garden.

"I discovered the place littered with dead trees and overgrown with weeds. I've done what my time here allows. I like to imagine I'm the princess now and this is my kingdom. See?" said Mary, pointing to the shells. "Over there is a seashore with my handsome young suitors queuing up to court me. These are my church bells, which will ring when I marry. And there are my maids-in-waiting, who will also be my bridesmaids. And woe betide them if any step out of line. I'll have their heads chopped off!"

Mary's giggle sent shivers down Alice's spine as these words were only too familiar in Wonderland.

Alice had now covered half the distance across the garden, even though normally it would have taken just a few strides. Perhaps Mary could answer more of her questions.

"Why does the house have no windows or doors? It must be terribly cold in winter."

"The weather doesn't change in this garden. Besides, it's a bit different inside. You'll see."

"Is there a fire in the hearth?" Although Alice was now warmed somewhat by the sun, she longed to feel the cosy heat of burning logs in a fireplace. She hoped Mary would offer her a hot drink too.

"How should I know?" said Mary, her mood changing. "I'm outside now and it's always different every time I go inside."

Alice felt Mary's answers raised more questions than they answered. She heard her mother's voice in her head: "Patience is a virtue, best served cold" or something like that. Then Mary spoke again.

"Parents think they know everything but they don't seem to realise the world has changed since their day and people need more than just sayings. Don't you agree, Alice?"

Alice had almost reached the door. She stretched out her hand to shake Mary's but to her amazement found her arm fell well short. She took a dozen more steps but still couldn't close the gap between them.

"Almost there, Alice. Do you know that word is spreading of your return to Wonderland? You're becoming quite the celebrity around town. Not that people here are very clever. Or nice. I hate the people in town. Everything will change for the better now you're here. We're going to have such lovely adventures together."

Alice was a little shocked at how Mary swung from snapping at her to befriending her. She really was quite contrary. However, there was one question Mary might be able to answer.

"Do you happen to know of something that's threatening Wonderland, Mary?"

"You mean the Jabberwocky? We all thought it was just a children's poem.

'Claws like knives, ending lives
Silent, unseen, swiftly, dead
Peace be carved by vorpal blade
As long as you can keep your head.'"

It was as Alice feared. Her very worst fears, in fact. The Jabberwocky had also returned to Wonderland and was poisoning it. Cheshire had spoken of terrible changes and a hidden terror. Surely they didn't expect *her* to seek out the vorpal blade and slay the monster? She walked on in silence until she had managed to put any thoughts of the Jabberwocky right out of her mind.

"It's peculiar," said Alice. "I remember everything about my earlier visit to Wonderland, but I haven't seen a single familiar face so far. Apart from talking to the Cheshire Cat,

I don't recognise anyone. The places even look different. Nothing's the same."

"Poor Alice. Are you sure it's not you that has changed?"

That was certainly true in many ways. Alice was no longer the childish girl who swam in her own tears, argued over tea with the Mad Hatter and threw tantrums in the royal court room. Yet that didn't explain why she hadn't met any of the same creatures this time round. Not that she wasn't glad to meet Mary, who seemed pleasant enough, albeit a little opinionated. There was something else slightly odd about Mary. She wore a fixed smile and fixed stare to match. Was it possible she wasn't telling Alice everything she knew?

Since talking to Cheshire and Mary, there was a new and bigger worry plaguing Alice; what if she were the cause of Wonderland's troubles? If her mere presence in Wonderland or her actions here were disturbing the natural equilibrium of things and making things worse? If so, that was another reason to leave this land as soon as possible. Alice took yet another step forward and collided into Mary, their foreheads bumping.

"Oh! I'm so sorry," exclaimed Alice.

"My fault. I should have reminded you to take the last steps more slowly because you never know who you're going to bump into."

The two girls stared into each other's faces until Mary suddenly leaned forward and kissed Alice on the cheek.

"I do hope we'll be the best of friends, Alice," said Mary, squeezing her so tightly it hurt a little. "Now come inside."

Based on the rundown exterior, Alice hadn't been expecting much as she stepped over the threshold, but she entered a dream come true. Inside, the house was one large room and it was everything Alice could have hoped for. Yellow flames lapped the inner walls of a large inglenook fireplace, crackling as they devoured logs as thick as Alice's body. A large silver-framed mirror hung on the wall over the fireplace. A deep red rug stretched from the hearth to the other side of the room where stood two leather armchairs and a sofa that looked so comfortable one could sleep on it, or rather in it. Brass oil lamps around the room threw light onto paintings of country landscapes. White lace curtains adorned lattice light windows which had mysteriously appeared in the open window spaces. A faint smell of soot mixed with freshly baked bread hung in the air. In some distant way, it reminded Alice of the Duchess's house (a frightening place from an earlier Wonderland adventure, where the cook threw plates and used too much pepper, and the Duchess nursed the baby). Yet this house was the cosiest, most peaceful one imaginable.

"Make yourself at home," said Mary with a smile. "It's all for you."

Behind Mary, the empty doorway was now blocked by a heavy wooden door held in place by big black metal hinges. Mary walked over to the fireplace and stood directly between Alice and the mirror. The funny thing was, looking past Mary, Alice could see both her own face and Mary's face in the mirror, even though by rights, Alice should only have seen the back of Mary's head. This was indeed a magical cottage. Alice was relieved to see it wasn't made of gingerbread.

She slumped into one of the leather armchairs as if her legs could no longer carry her. The chair seemed to fold her in a loving embrace. On a small table next to the chair was some cake, fruit and a glass of milk. At a nod from Mary, Alice helped herself. She ate and drank while listening to Mary talk about how the house would magically change itself to make visitors feel at home. Alice was both surprised and relieved that Mary hadn't quizzed her about all the things she had got up to during her time in Wonderland.

Mary also talked about the people in the nearby town, mostly how much older, stupider and unpleasant they were. And how good it was at last to have someone as smart and sensible as Alice to talk to. It was probably the combination of being in a warm, dry room, Mary's sing-song voice and her own exhaustion, but within two minutes Alice was fast asleep.

Alice knew she was dreaming but this didn't seem to diminish the abject horror of her nightmare.

She dreamt she was in the Queen of Hearts' garden playing croquet with the courtiers. Everyone was having fun, when all at once, the head and haunches of a large beast appeared above the brow of a hill above them. A huge tiger came into view and loped slowly down the hill towards them. Nobody else had seen the predator and Alice was in two minds whether to run and make sure she escaped or to make others aware of the danger and jeopardise her own flight. She decided in favour of warning others. As people

71

screamed and scattered to safety, the tiger began to charge down the hill. Alice turned and ran for her life.

Despite the nightmare, Alice woke refreshed. There was no way of telling how long she had slept although new logs in the hearth suggested it had been several hours. There was no sign of Mary. Alice was sure she had regained all her memories. At least, she couldn't think of anything that she'd forgotten, apart from how she'd acquired the feather, that is.

She lolled in the armchair and went over recent events in her head, especially her conversation with the Cheshire Cat. She had to get back home as fast as she could but she would be more than happy to help the creatures of Wonderland at the same time if she could. Even happier should it aid her quest. However, the idea of having to battle the Jabberwocky was something she intended to avoid at all cost. She very much hoped their paths wouldn't cross but she suspected they might, somewhere near the end of her journey if she wasn't mistaken. *Hope for the best, plan for the worst, said the voice in her head.*

A few moments could turn into years if one wasn't careful. Alice rose reluctantly yet feeling like a whole different person. She was ready for anything (except the Jabberwocky). What a shame she hadn't woken up in her own world, suitcase packed and her father on the mend. True, this was a wonderful adventure and she had made a new friend in Mary and had all kinds of adventures. But did everything have to be so serious and gloomy here? The old Wonderland had been more carefree. Had her own life changed that much? Of course it had. She was no longer a child. She had finished school and was moving away from home. Almost overnight, everyone had gone from telling her not to grow up too fast, to grow up and take more responsibility. Older people shook their heads at her in dismay when she expressed opinions different to their generation. They said she was bright enough but lacked experience and wisdom. Alice knew it was just because they were frightened of change and jealous of her youth. *I'm sure Mary would hate "them"*, she said to herself.

It was then she noticed a small back door in the rear wall. It was unimposing, which was why she hadn't noticed it earlier. On the other hand, it looked out of place compared to the rest of room. For that reason alone, Alice understood that it was the door she was supposed to take. She considered stepping out of the front door first, just to check her surroundings, but knew that even should she be able to re-enter the house, it might well take an hour or two's walking to get back in!

Fed and rested, Alice opened the back door, stepped out and looked out across the decorative back garden. Looking farther afield, to the path and beyond, she was pleased to see a small group of buildings two or three miles away. Her heart sank when she realised it would take her the best part of a day to reach there, judging by the distances she had managed to cover of late. A part of her wanted to run back to that comfy armchair and curl up in front of the fire. She was sure she would find a fresh glass of milk and more food there. Another part heard a nagging parental voice: "You can have too much of a good thing. Everything in moderation."

Gingerly, she followed a line of paving stones that connected the back door to the main path and was both surprised and delighted to find she could cross the garden at her normal pace. She made excellent progress on the path too. Mary had been right. Leaving Halfway House was easier. What Alice didn't know was that she had been in Halfway House for two whole days.

The sky above was deep blue and what clouds there were, were large fluffy ones. It was warm outside but thankfully the clammy, suffocating air of the moors had gone. The rules that governed walking were back to normal, at least normal for Alice. After the frustration of trying to get to the cottage, Alice felt like she simply flew along as she headed towards the next dwellings, which had begun to look very much like a farm.

A little further along the path, a dry-stone wall cut the land in two. A kissing gate straddled the path. It seemed that on this side of the wall were the moors and on the other farmland. Alice felt somehow lighter as she passed through the gate and left the diseased marshlands. She decided to name the kissing gate, Moorgate.

The closer she got to the farm, the more fertile the land became. At first, clumps of grass sprouted randomly along the path. Then taller plants and bushes lined the way. Eventually, she caught sight of tilled land and fields of wheat through gaps in the hedges.

Up until now, the path had run as straight as an arrow, from the base of the weir, through the Winter Forest and right across the marshland. Now, after Moorgate, it began to twist and turn, the way forward increasingly obstructed by tall hedgerows. On rounding a bend, Alice was met with a collection of stone houses and wooden outbuildings. It was indeed a farm and not ten feet away in front of her was an angry dog baring its teeth, growling at her as if it meant to tear her limb from limb.

"Have you milked pigs before?" asked Mrs MacDonald.

"I can't say I have, no," said Alice.

"Can you say you haven't?"

"Yes."

"Then why don't you talk about what you can say rather than talk about what you can't say?"

CHAPTER 4

THE FUNNY FARM

Alice froze in terror as a long line of saliva dripped from one of the dog's curved incisors.

"Is that you, Alice? Goodness me. It's me, Colonel Pavlov from the train! Remember? Oh, I do apologise, I'm drooling." Pavlov was also whispering as though he was afraid someone would overhear him.

Alice was flabbergasted. She had never seen an animal go from being ferocious to timid quite so quickly. And she certainly hadn't expected a beast that was about to tear her to shreds to suddenly introduce itself. Then she found her tongue.

"Pavlov? How did you end up here? You took a completely different road to me. And why are you whispering?"

"My owners don't like me to talk. They get angry and beat me if I do. Or worse. Please don't tell them you heard me talking." Now cowering, Pavlov looked very different to the bossy bloodhound Alice had met on the train. The Pavlov Alice had met then was clearly used to giving orders rather than taking them. He had even helped get her and other passengers off the train. Not this Pavlov. With whiskers greyer and eyes more bloodshot than before, he was looking his age.

"Of course, I won't. How horrible for you. But why do they treat you like an animal?" Alice at once realised how silly this question must have sounded.

"They treat all animals badly on this farm."

"What keeps you here then?"

In answer, Pavlov shook his head and rattled a heavy piece of chain around his neck. The other end of the chain was fastened to a kennel in the middle of the yard, which allowed Pavlov enough freedom to guard the buildings but not to venture off the property. *How beastly*, thought Alice. *Reduced from the rank of Colonel to guard duty.*

Alice noticed that Pavlov's tail was somewhat shorter and had a bandage wrapped around the end.

"Did they do that to you?"

"It's not so bad. You know what they say," said Pavlov. "'What doesn't kill you, makes you stronger'."

He growled quietly but both of them knew he had little spirit left in him.

"You were so distinguished when I met you on the train. And more than a little gruff. You can be quite intimidating, you know, though I know you don't mean to be."

Pavlov straightened up with pride for a brief moment, then sank back down on his haunches. "You're right, of course. It's mostly show. My bark's worse than my bite. If truth be known, I haven't bitten a soul outside conflict. I haven't the stomach for it."

"In that case, it's very brave of you to guard this place."

"Not really. Although, do you know what the soldiers used to say about me in the war? 'It's not the size of the dog in a fight, it's the size of the fight in the dog.'"

Alice wasn't sure whether Pavlov could even muster up a friendly argument in his current state. But she knew he liked talking about his time in the army.

"What war did you fight in?"

"Oh lots. The Furry Years War … the Pawleonic Wars, that was where we tore a bone apart … the Battle of Gruffalgar, that was a tough one. And, of course, the Boxer Rebellion."

"Goodness. That's a lot. I can't say I've heard of them all."

"No, you wouldn't. It was all very secret. They called us the hush puppies."

"So what happened to you after you ran off? How did you end up like this?"

"It's a long story, Alice."

"It can't be that long, I saw you just a day or so ago?"

"More like a year or two. In dog years that's about fourteen years, you know. I always wondered what happened to you at Alice Falls."

Two years? No wonder Pavlov looked older. Alice's head reeled as her brain tried to come to terms with the fact that two years had passed since their fall at the weir. Then she told herself anything could happen in Wonderland. Perhaps time passed differently for different creatures, or she had slept in the cottage longer than she realised. She asked Pavlov to tell his story.

"Here's the short version," said Pavlov in a low voice. "It seems war veterans are not in great demand on the job market so I worked as a security guard for a while. I kept my nose down, if not entirely clean, and also had a string of jobs in debt collection hounding people for money."

"Poor you. It can't have been much fun having to badger people."

"I hounded I didn't badger."

"What's the difference?"

"A couple of stripes. Higher rank, you know. Anyway, out of the blue I got a new lead and became the companion of an old lady called May Hubart. Who says you can't teach an old dog new tricks? At first, it was fine. All I had to do was to keep her company and make sure none of the silverware went missing. She had a few children, quite late in her life – hence people called her Old Mother Hubart - but they had left home young. She gave them all her money in the hope they'd return home but they just squandered her fortune. She had to sell most of her assets, including the big house. We moved into a run-down cottage where we lived hand to paw. One day, she went to the cupboard and there was no more food. I almost died of hunger before she got hold of a loaf or two of bread. She was convinced I was at death's door and even had a coffin made for me. That was when we fell out and she began to treat me like a pet. Man's best friend I may be but apparently not woman's. Not long after she sold me to this farmer who, as she put it, 'Would knock some sense into me'. It's hard to forgive that."

"They do say every dog has its day."

"I think my days are all in the past."

Out of nowhere came an angry shout. "Rex! Come here you good-for-nothing cur!"

"I must go. Take care, Alice. I hope to see you again."

"Rex? Is that what they call you now?"

Pavlov didn't answer. The look in his big brown bloodshot eyes said it all.

"Who's there? Who is it? Come into the light." The cry came from a large, buxom woman, who was standing in the farmhouse doorway.

"My name's Alice. Sorry if I startled you."

"I'm more surprised you didn't startle Rex. He usually barks his head off at anything that moves. Only thing he's good for, the useless mutt."

Alice so wanted to help Pavlov. He deserved better, so she spoke up.

"His name is Colonel Pavlov."

"What? Pavlov? Don't be silly. He's always been Rex. At least, that's what he answers to."

I'm sure I would answer to Rex too if I were kept on a chain and beaten, thought Alice, but decided against speaking her mind. She was sure Pavlov, as an ex-soldier, would agree that one had to choose one's battles. And now was probably not the time or the place.

The woman was clearly the farmer's wife as she had a round, weather-beaten face with rosy cheeks. Over a blue chequered dress she wore a white apron that was spattered with flour and stained red in places. The impression that she had been cooking was reinforced by the fact that she was carrying a rolling pin in one hand and a carving knife in the other.

"Why you're just a child! Come in and have a slice of plum pie. What on earth are you doing way out here on your lonesome? My name's Mrs MacDonald, the farmer's wife. You can call me Mrs. M. Now tell me what you've been up to."

Mrs MacDonald cut Alice a large slice of red plum pie with the carving knife. Its blade dripped red juice onto her apron. Alice had neither the strength nor inclination to tell her host about trains in rivers, talking animals and a magic cottage in the wilderness, so in between mouthfuls of plum pie and gulps of apple juice, she explained that she had become lost while picking wild blackberries and was trying to find her way back to town.

"Well you're jolly lucky you found us then. The mud flats are home to the Eelers. They hunt for girls like you. Don't you worry, we'll look after you and make sure you get home safely."

Alice had seen those dark, ghoulish fishermen on the moors, but for the life of her she couldn't work out how she had managed to guess their name right. She was also more than a little surprised that the farmer's wife was being so kind to her and had not been the monster Alice had expected. After all, how could anyone who mistreated their dog not be a beast themselves? And this pie did taste very good.

"This is exquisite plum pie. You're a very good cook, Mrs M."

"Thank you, my dear. Very nice of you to say so. I made a batch of them for my children."

"Oh, are they here?"

The woman gave Alice a hurt look that melted into an expression of sad forgiveness.

"No, not at the moment, dear. I have two children, Gillian and Jackson. Jackson is one of the town councillors, you know. He's become a very big figure around town. He's so busy he doesn't have time to visit me much. You probably know him if you're from Banbury. He'd be quite a catch for a girl like you."

Alice wasn't at all thrilled at what the farmer's wife was suggesting. The woman had also put a little too much stress on the word "if", implying she didn't believe Alice was from town. The word "Jackson" rang a bell in Alice's head, but she couldn't say why. Perhaps she had had a tutor called Jackson and it was a school bell she was hearing.

"Gillian left home around the same time as Jackson. She's probably married to the town physician, Doctor Foster, by now. Most likely has a family of her own, I wouldn't wonder. I'm sure she'll come for a visit soon."

Alice sensed that the farmer's wife hadn't seen her children for a very long time. There was an awkward silence, which Mrs MacDonald eventually broke. "So where are your blackberries?"

"I didn't find any."

"That's because there aren't any blackberries in these parts." Mrs MacDonald smiled frostily at Alice.

"That must be the reason I lost my way then," said Alice, "Through walking so far trying to find some." It was Alice's turn to look smug.

"Lost your way?" said the farmer's wife, disbelievingly. "You can't lose what you never had, my dear."

There was another long moment when neither spoke.

"Anyway," said Mrs MacDonald at length, "if you were wandering in the mud flats, it might be good for you to know that breathing in that polluted air takes away your dearest memories. No wonder you can't find your way back home. The flats will have taken away your most precious memory. People say it's the toll you have to pay for crossing the home of the Eelers."

It was true, Alice had temporarily forgotten the urgency to get back home, even her family and everyone she had met and everything she had done in Wonderland. But since she couldn't think of anything else important that she may have forgotten, she was sure her memory was now intact and that Mrs M's alleged curse of the moor was just an old wives' tale. There was another silence, during which the farmer's wife went to a cot in the corner of the room and gave it a heavy-handed rock.

"Is that your baby? Can I see?"

"Please don't," said Mrs MacDonald a little too quickly. "She's sleeping." An untanned pelt, once white but now dirty and by the look of things also stained with plum juice, was draped over the cot. The farmer's wife tucked it in tighter round the edges, humming the lullaby "Hush Little Baby".

"You won't believe what we've done to stop the baby crying," said the woman, giving Alice a long sideways stare. Alice didn't want to hazard a guess what they had had to do but since this was Wonderland, she feared it may have involved white rabbits.

"Is Mr MacDonald around to help?"

"Ha!" The farmer's wife snorted once out loud angrily, waving the carving knife in the air. "The baby's father is out. More likely than not clowning around instead of hunting for skins for the cot. You won't believe how much blood, sweat and tears it needs to stop that baby crying."

Although the farmer's wife tried to smile at Alice, she could see the woman's eyes well up with tears as her jaw set in rage. Alice thought it best not to ask anything about the baby or its father. She also decided that she had outstayed her welcome. She had to get going. However, before she could excuse herself and leave, the farmer's wife reappeared at Alice's side, jollier than ever. "Would you like to help me milk the pigs, dear?"

"Don't you mean the cows?"

"We don't have any cows. What a funny little girl you are!" And she pinched Alice's cheek hard.

The farmer's wife began to lead Alice by the hand to the pig pen.

"Do you really need the carving knife to go milking?" asked Alice.

"Probably not. But better safe than sorry."

It seemed an interesting interpretation of the word "safe".

On the way to the pig pen, Alice caught a glimpse of Colonel Pavlov's paws protruding from his kennel. She wanted to shout 'hello' to him but followed her instinct to let sleeping dogs lie.

"Have you milked pigs before?"

"I can't say I have, no," said Alice.

"Can you say you haven't?"

"Yes."

"Then why don't you talk about what you can say rather than talk about what you can't say? You're the most peculiar, adorable child I've met, you know. I could squeeze you to bits."

The farmer's wife smiled knowingly at Alice, who tried to keep a healthy distance between them as they crossed the farmyard to a rather smelly pen in the far corner.

"In the beginning, I used to have four piglets, you know. Now I only have the three pigs."

"What happened to the other one?"

"Other two you mean."

"Four minus three equals one, I think you'll find."

"Not if you add one extra pig. Do keep up, Alice! Now, our first pig we sent to the market in town."

"To sell the milk?"

"I can't imagine rashers of bacon being able to sell much of anything, can you? Now 'sell *for* much' is a different kettle of fish entirely. We did very well out of that pig.

Anyway, the second pig we kept. Pig number three ran away and opened a steak house in Banbury."

Alice giggled and tried to turn it into a cough so as not to appear rude.

"Pig number four we ignored totally but she stuck around anyway. I thought about making a silk purse out of her ears but she wouldn't hear a word of it. Then one day in trotted the ugliest pig you ever did see, squealing like...well, a stuck pig. I felt so sorry for it I decided to add it to my collection. When it arrived, it moaned about everything under the sun – the food, the bedding, being chained to the fence - but I soon put a stop to that. He won't talk again, I'll tell you that for nothing!"

Alice looked inside the pig pen. Two pink pigs, one fat and one which looked neglected, stared at her in seeming despair. The third pig, which was grey and much hairier, had its hind quarters towards Alice.

"Hoy! Ugly pig! Come here, we have a guest," shouted the farmer's wife and hurled a stone at the pig's rump. The animal turned its head around and Alice saw that it was Chester, the wart-hog from the train. Dirtier, thinner and extremely dejected.

"What did I tell you! The ugliest pig you ever did see. He doesn't produce much milk either."

Chester's eyes opened wider and he stared forlornly at the muddy ground. Alice used a hand to stifle a cry. For all his grumpiness, Chester didn't deserve this fate. The farmer's wife took Alice's reaction as repulsion at Chester's appearance.

"Disgusting aren't they? Let's not milk the pigs. Come and help me look for my cat in the barn."

"I really should be going. It's quite a long walk back."

"I thought you said you were lost?"

"I think I can remember the way back now. I guess the effect of the mud flats has worn off."

"Honey catches more flies than vinegar with you, doesn't it, my dear Alice? Well, you can't leave just yet. You need to work off all that plum pie you ate. Don't want you getting fat. At least, not too quickly."

Alice didn't relish the idea of being shut up in a barn with Mrs M. "How about we take a quick look at your fields?"

"Why? Nothing happening in the fields, I'm afraid. Sadly all our crops burnt."

"How terrible. Was it a forest fire?" asked Alice, doubting that there was such a thing as a field fire.

"No. We burnt the fields ourselves to get rid of the infestation."

"Was it an infestation of rats?"

"Ladybirds mainly. Other creatures too; dormice, bees, corn buntings, hares, spiders, wagtails, dragonflies, you name it. But mainly ladybirds. Crawling with the nasty things. Chattering all the time. The idea was that we would burn their homes, they would go back to look for their children, who of course would have fled or would be in hiding, and the parents would get so distraught they would voluntarily relocate. It was the most humane way we could think of. Well it worked a treat. The downside is we have lost half our livelihood but it's a small price to pay for ending the pestilence."

Alice decided Mrs M was quite mad. And possibly dangerous.

There was an empty field off to the left with a drinking trough in it and wire fencing around. Alice asked Mrs M what animals she kept there. Instead of a direct answer, the woman gave Alice a long and distrusting look and said, "Have you seen Mary?"

Alice didn't like lying because she didn't like other people doing it to her. Even though she counted her story about collecting berries as a white lie, she had made her blackberry bed and now had to lie in it.

"Mary who?" she said unconvincingly.

"Mary Peep. Probably about your height." The farmer's wife stared into Alice's eyes intensely. "People call her 'Bow Peep' on account of the bows in her hair."

"Well I don't have bows in my hair. And I'm afraid I don't know any Bow Peep," said Alice, who didn't see this as lying as she couldn't say for sure if the Mary she had met at the cottage was the same one they called Bow Peep.

"Have you seen her?" Alice asked Mrs M.

"No. But apparently she took my sheep to Shepherd's Bush. She was supposed to bring them back and put them in this pen. Rumour has it that she lost them and is hoping that they'll find their own way back. Stupid girl! Well if they do come back, I shall probably have to cut off their tails to teach them a lesson. I'll hang them on the branches of trees as a warning to my other animals."

Alice thought it was quite awful how Mrs M went around cutting off tails.

"And as for Mary, well there's a new pillory in the market square that would fit her just nicely," said Mrs MacDonald, staring at Alice's neck.

"I do hope you get your sheep back. Have you any other animals on the farm apart from the pigs?"

The farmer's wife teared up again and stared into the distance. "I used to have horses and cows and sheep and hens. And lizards and elephants. And a pangolin. I trained them all to stop talking and obey me. Animals are so much better than people, you know. Won't leave you if you show them who's boss.

"I loved them so much. All gone now. I blame those children of mine. Jackson used to sleep under the haystacks instead of looking after the cows and sheep. He looked so sweet dressed in his blue shirt and trousers and carrying that trumpet of his. He used to try to call the cattle and sheep by playing his trumpet. He played so badly that more often than not, the animals ran away into the meadow and cornfields." Mrs MacDonald bucked up. "He's very successful nowadays though, did I tell you? Town official no less. I'll bet everybody's terrified of him."

"I had to flog the horses," Mrs MacDonald said at length, her mood plunging again.

"Sell them?"

"No, whip them. They wouldn't clean the lake. They all drowned in the end."

"How awful."

"Just shows. You can lead a horse to water but you can't make him swim. Well, not for hours on end at any rate. The farmhands were to blame for some of the animals leaving. We hired that dunce, Humphrey Dunfry, the neighbour's child to mind the hens. Something wrong in his head, that lad. He used to collect the eggs and carry them around in his pockets. You can guess what happened to most of the eggs. The hens were so distraught they flew off first chance they had."

"I didn't know hens were good at flying."

"You'd be surprised what you're capable of when you've been cooped up too long," said Mrs MacDonald, brandishing the knife. "Even pigs can fly if they've the will and wherefore. They wrote a poem about it:

"Inkle oinkle little pig
Why d'you always grow so big.
Soon you won't fit in your sty,
Spread your trotters, start to fly."

Mrs MacDonald finished her peculiar poem just as they reached the barn.

"Here we are. Now do be careful not to let the mice out. You know what they say mice do when the cat's away. Anyway, the mice are not well at the moment."

They entered and Alice did as she was told by closing the barn door quickly behind her. It was a lovely old barn with haystacks, pitchforks and golden beams of sunlight coming in through cracks in the wooden walls.

"Now, you have a look for my cat," said Mrs MacDonald. "I'll just go and get the bread bin to put it in."

Alice was happy to be left alone but not so happy to hear the farmer's wife bolt the barn door from the outside. As the woman's footsteps retreated, Alice tried the door but it wouldn't budge. She turned to see if there was another way out but there was no second exit and no loose planks. She hoped the cat was indeed somewhere in the barn as Mrs M had mentioned mice and Alice disliked mice intensely.

At the back of the barn were a hundred or so bales of hay stacked willy nilly on top of each other. Gingerly, afraid she might uncover a nest of mice, Alice moved some of the loose bales in the hope of finding Mrs M's missing cat. Within a few minutes, Alice was hot and bothered and sat down on some straw to rest. In next to no time, she was sound asleep.

As Alice slept, her nightmare about the tiger continued from where it had left off at Halfway House.

The tiger had begun running down the hill towards Alice and the courtiers. Alice turned and headed for a stone chapel she spied in the corner of the Queen's garden. She reasoned that the tiger was more likely to hunt prey in the open garden before it ventured inside a building.

The chapel turned out to be a large mediaeval banquet room on the inside, empty apart from one long wooden table and some benches. Alice stepped up onto a bench and then the table, just in case the tiger decided to enter the room. By now, a steady stream of terrified people had followed Alice into the chapel. They milled around, trying to comfort one another by agreeing that they had found safe shelter. Not long after, however, the tiger slowly crept into the chapel and fixed Alice with a malicious stare. Though still large and scrawny, the tiger had somehow lost its stripes. Alice knew that this was one reason the tiger was so angry but as to why it should blame her for this, she had no clue. It prowled round and round the table, taking swipes with a huge paw at people unlucky enough to be within reach.

Alice suddenly realised she wasn't safe as the tiger could easily jump up onto the table. She pinched herself hard in an attempt to wake herself from the dream but to no avail. She tried to shout and scream in a bid to end her nightmare but no sound escaped her lips. The tiger gave an evil smile as if it knew Alice was trapped in her dream. Not long now.

Alice woke with a start and saw Mrs MacDonald standing in front of her with a knife in her hand. Thankfully, she was not facing Alice. Flattened against the far wall of the barn were three large grey mice huddled together. They were frightened out of their lives. Despite them being the size of dogs, Alice felt pity rather than fear.

"Poor little things," exclaimed Alice. "What's wrong with them?"

"I had to cut off their tails with this knife and they haven't grown back yet."

"I very much doubt they will," said a horrified Alice. "Am I right in assuming these mice are also blind and you cut off their tails with a carving knife because you thought that they were chasing you?"

"They're not blind in the sense you mean. I mean, I don't go around mutilating sight-impaired field mice. What kind of monster do you think I am? No, what happened was, they wouldn't leave the fields even after I'd burnt down their houses. I reasoned with them but they just didn't see my point of view. So in that sense, they were blind to reason. I just thought that they might not be so attached to the fields if they weren't attached to their tails. Hasn't worked though. They just stay huddled there in the corner."

"Wouldn't they leave now if you left the barn door open?"

The three mice nodded their heads excitedly and squeaked the word 'yes' over and over again.

"Possibly, but I want to nurse them back to full health first before I let them back into the wild. That's the least I can do for them." There was a resounding clang as the farmer's wife slid the thick metal bolt across the inside of the barn doors to lock them all in.

"You're not trying to talk again, are you?" she asked the mice. They shook their heads violently. "Good, because I wouldn't want to have to cut off any other parts." She turned to Alice. "I was wondering Alice, how are you at catching rats, mice and other rodents?"

The three mice looked in panic at Alice.

"Not good at all. I have a cat, Dinah. She is capital at catching mice."

The mice looked as though their eyes would pop out.

"But she's not here. And I'm useless at that kind of thing." Alice was talking more to the mice, who both visibly and audibly gave a collective sigh of relief.

"Shame," said Mrs MacDonald. "You see my cat's gone missing. Not the first time. And one can't run a farm without a cat."

Or without crops and livestock, Alice almost said, but just managed to swallow the words back down in time. She thought the word "livestock" may have got caught just below her epiglottis, but she was confident it wasn't going to get out.

"The cat went missing twice before. The first time was right after I clipped its tail for talking. It had apparently travelled all the way to London just to catch sight of royalty. It shouldn't have done that."

A cat may look at a king, thought Alice, recalling one of Cheshire's remarks.

"It got into the palace through an open window but all it saw was a royal mouse under the throne. Complete waste of time if you ask me as there are plenty of mice here.

"The second time it skulked away in mid-winter to this barn to have a litter of kittens. Terrible fuss that was. It was so cold I had to knit gloves and scarves for the three kittens so that they would keep warm and their mother could get back to work, catching my mice. Do you think they were grateful? The stupid kittens were so careless with their new clothes – lost them, found them, soiled them, washed them, lost, found, soil, wash – you get the picture. The mother cat was so busy it didn't catch any mice for over a month."

"And now your cat's gone missing again?"

"Not so much missing as presumed dead. I saw two boys from town in the farmyard the other day. One of them, that tearaway Johnny Thin, was trying to throw my cat down the well just because it was a good mouse-catcher. You see, the boys come here trying to catch mice for themselves. Some townsfolk are so hungry down at the market, they'll exchange anything for a string of mice."

Alice screwed up her nose in disgust. "Was the other boy called Tommy Stout?"

"Thomas as I recall, yes. His father, Peter Stout, is one of the town councillors and plays the flute."

"Then I shouldn't worry yourself too much. I do believe Thomas Stout may have pulled your cat out of the well."

"I'm not sure if that's such good news."

"Surely it's good if he saved your cat from drowning?"

"Not when you think that a nice plump cat sells for a barrowful of firewood in the marketplace."

"He wouldn't sell your cat would he?"

"He'd sell his grandmother if she were plumper. And alive. Once he stole a tray of fresh piggy doughnuts I'd put on the window sill, the knave! I caught him running down the street eating them and beat the daylights out of him till he saw stars. I also made him come back and play his father's flute for us all. He could only play one song "O'er the hills and far away". Trouble is he played it so well, everyone stopped work to listen. Then they felt compelled to dance. Couldn't stop themselves. My children, the neighbours, the farmhands, even the animals started to dance. People stopped work, broke things and laughed until their sides split. Possessed they were! Rumour has it his father played the flute so well he could make people follow him out into the hills. The man's working in Germany if I'm not mistaken."

Alice felt there must be some rhyme or reason to everything she had heard, seen and done in Wonderland.

But for the life of her she couldn't make head or tail of it. Some, if not all of the animals she had met on the train had ended up in appalling conditions. Colonel Pavlov, the dog, and Chester, the wart-hog were older, helpless and vulnerable. Other animals, like the pigs, cat, mice and wildlife didn't seem much better off. Of one thing she was certain, the farmer's wife was mistreating the animals here; animals that could talk and had feelings. It was as if the woman were trying to build some strange menagerie. But why? So her children would return home? To keep her company? What did she have in the cot and where was Mr MacDonald? And why was she trying to keep Alice there? Alice realised she must leave at once for her own safety. And if she were ever to find her way back home.

"You have been a marvellous host, Mrs M. So kind. And I don't know what you put in your plum pie but it's the best I've ever had. But now I simply must be going or my parents shall wonder where I've got to."

"Can't you wait until Mr MacDonald gets back? He won't be long now. It would be a little rude of you not to stay and say hello. I'm sure he's dying to meet the Alice everyone is talking about."

Alice suspected there was quite a bit of dying whenever the farmer showed up. She reached to unbolt the barn door.

"Very well," said the farmer's wife. "One little game before you go. One question about the mud flats. If you answer it correctly, you can return home right away. But if you get it wrong, then you have another piece of plum pie before you leave. Is that a deal?"

Alice knew she should simply decline and go but she didn't want to be rude to her host. What could be the harm in humouring the woman with her riddle? Surely the worst that could happen is she would have to eat another slice of that delicious pie. Alice might have thought twice had she seen the frantic gestures of the mice behind her. She might have made a dash for the door had she heard them whispering "You can't have your cake and eat it". But as she didn't, she agreed. And the farmer's wife asked her riddle. It was about the mud flats Alice had just escaped from.

"As I was going to the flats, I met a dog with seven cats.
Each cat had seven rats.
Each rat had seven mice.
Each mouse had seven lice.
Lice, mice, rats and cats,
How many were there going to the flats?"

Alice had heard something like this before and knew there was a catch. The obvious answer was to calculate all the creatures together – something to the power of something, no doubt. The farmer's wife grinned and waved her carving knife about, presumably preparing to cut another slice of plum pie. Then Alice remembered how to answer the conundrum.

"It depends. If they are all coming the opposite way, *from* the mud flats, then there was just one going there. Me."

The farmer's wife went red in the face and clearly wanted to throttle Alice for ruining her plans, whatever they were.

"Now," said Alice, "you promised to let me go."

"Promises are like pie crusts, made to be broken." Then a smile slowly spread across Mrs MacDonald's face and her eyes widened in malice. "Anyway, they weren't coming the other way. They were going the *same* way as you? How many were there?" It was a last-ditch attempt to prevent Alice from leaving.

"Then that would be 2,802: one dog, seven cats, forty-nine rats, three hundred and forty-three mice and two thousand four hundred and one lice. Plus me."

Alice found herself almost able to forgive old Mr Barnett, her maths tutor, for rapping her knuckles every time she got her sums wrong.

"But what I really don't understand," she continued, "is why they weren't fighting amongst themselves because they would, you know. Cats and rats are not friends at the best of times."

The farmer's wife let out a yowl and looked up at the rafters as if trying to bring them crashing down on Alice.

Seeing her chance, Alice unbolted the barn door and bolted out. The farmer's wife gave chase but the three mice dived between the woman's ankles, causing her to stumble. Alice raced across the courtyard and out of the gate towards the road. The farmer's wife was in hot pursuit, brandishing her knife. But just as she was gaining on Alice, she tripped over a chain, which had been pulled tight between the kennel and a defiant-looking Colonel Pavlov.

The sheep pulled an even longer face than she already had and her spectacles almost slipped off her nose. "It's the perfect camouflage. Who would suspect a sheep of dressing up as a wolf?" Her voice shook and cracked as she whispered.

"Who indeed?"

CHAPTER 5

ALL ABOUT TOWN

Alice didn't stop running until she was sure the farmer's wife was no longer chasing her. When she did stop, she discovered that she was on a different-looking road to the one she had arrived on. She wasn't quite sure if it was the right road, but she remembered the Cheshire Cat having once told her that if she had no specific destination in mind, then any road would get her there.

The road wound to the right up ahead and above a tall hedge Alice could see the steeple of a distant church. *That must be Banbury*, thought Alice, and decided it was a far safer place than the troubled farm.

After a couple more bends, the sandy road rose gently and straddled a small stone bridge that crossed a stream, which chuckled and sparkled in the sun. On the low wall of the bridge sat a rather portly man. It was difficult to spot where his head ended and his body started. His cheeks and chins were unshaven and clothes in tatters. His short legs, tapering from thick at the top to thin at the ankles, dangled over the edge of the wall like upside down dunce's caps. Alice guessed immediately it was Humphrey Dunfry, the child the farmer's wife had asked to mind the hens. But this was no child. He had grown up.

"Are you hungry?" asked the man as Alice drew level with him.

"Not particularly, thank you," replied Alice.

"I have lots of eggs. I can give you one if you want."

Alice saw that both pockets of Humphrey's once-white trousers were stained yellowy-green, the consequence of years of unsuccessfully carrying hen's eggs around in his pockets. He smelled rotten. It looked as if the knocks and bruises of life had left him a broken man and nobody had helped him to pick up the pieces. Least of all Mrs M, who had sent him packing.

"Is your name Mary?" he asked.

"No."

"Oh. You look like a Mary to me. I get so confused these days. I'm Humphrey Dunfry. What did you say your name was?"

"Alice."

"Did you? I don't remember you telling me. Maybe I remembered that you were about to tell me. A liar should have a good memory, you know, but as I don't tell lies, my memory sometimes fails me. It's all because I used to go to the mud flats. It eats your memories, you know. Do you have a good memory?"

"Yes, I believe so. Or I used to until recently."

"Oh," said Humphrey, in a way that implied he thought Alice told lies.

"But I don't tell lies."

Humphrey looked very confused. "But if you do tell lies, maybe you told me one now, when you said you don't lie."

"That's a good point. But on the other hand, how do I know you weren't lying? Perhaps you were just pretending to have a bad memory." Was Humphrey as sharp as a knife in reality? A second look at him told Alice he wasn't. She felt sorry for him and thought she'd better cheer him up.

"It's a shame you couldn't stay at the farm, Humphrey. Mrs MacDonald said that all the hens flew away, so I suppose there were no more eggs for you to collect."

"The hens didn't fly away. She cut off their heads. One day, she was telling me about the curse of the mud flats. I said 'curses are like hens, they both come home to roost'. She got it into her head that her hens were cursed and that was that. Out came the carving knife. The headless hens still laid eggs for months afterwards but the eggs came out with their tops already cut off."

"How convenient," said Alice, again looking on the bright side. She liked boiled eggs but always found cutting the tops off very difficult.

As Humphrey conjured up images of his days at the farm, he sucked on his soiled shirt sleeves.

"I wish there was something I could do to help you," Alice said, thinking out loud.

Humphrey gave a small but kind smile as if he appreciated her concern.

"Oh," he said, "don't worry about me. I've survived just fine so far. You need to worry more about yourself. That's what I say. Home again, home again, jiggedy-jig."

Humphrey looked Alice straight in the eye and said in a deadly serious voice. "While you still can."

"What do you mean?" she asked, not sure if she should take advice from a man with egg on his face.

"These days, the best way to help anyone in Wonderland is to look after yourself. Look after the chicks and the hens will look after themselves and all that. And if you're wondering, the egg came first."

Despite the fact that Humphrey was just a shell of a man and as crazy as a soup sandwich, something told Alice he might give her a clue as to how to return home.

"Why did you carry eggs around in your pockets?"

"Any fool knows that you never put all your eggs in one basket. And since Mrs MacDonald only had one basket, I had to use my brains."

"Right. Have you ever thought about washing your clothes?"

"I'm not as stupid as I look, you know. Only a fool would wash his dirty laundry in public."

Alice thought Humphrey might like to help her rescue Pavlov, Chester and the other farm animals.

"I know you worked at the farm once upon a time. I'm sure you loved the animals. How would you like to go back there and help me rescue them?" said Alice. "They are suffering terribly."

"You can't help everyone, you know, Alice. Sometimes you just need to walk away, even if you fall. That's my philosophy on life."

"I'm not sure I should walk away. Or even want to. I feel somehow responsible for the animals. Maybe you should too."

"No one said looking the other way is easy," said Humphrey sadly. "I'm sure you've heard the saying 'sometimes you have to be cruel to be kind'. Well that's what you should do to children and animals to help them stand on their own two feet. Worked for me."

Even ignoring the fact that Humphrey wasn't standing, and that most animals had four feet, Alice was sure that being neglected had not helped him one bit.

"Spare the rod and spoil the child," he continued. "Too much mollycoddling and I could have easily ended up a bad egg, you know."

Alice was getting tired of people asking her to live according to proverbs and Humphrey seemed obsessed with them.

"Well, I'm sorry you've had a hard life. But not everyone is nasty." Not to the degree that the farmer's wife was at any rate. "My parents aren't unkind, in any case. I'm sure they think everything they do and say is for my own good."

"Which is the reason you are in the predicament you are in now. A sterner upbringing may have kept you on the straight and narrow, instead of being on this windy lane. You can't make an omelette without breaking eggs, you know. Why are you being so facetious?"

"Am I being facetious?"

"Probably not. I don't know what the word means. I just like it because all the words are in the right order alphabetically."

It was true that Alice had had a more sheltered upbringing than most other children she knew. She rather took it for granted that her parents were always there for her and couldn't imagine how unbearable life would be without them. Or with a mother like Mrs MacDonald.

"Well, I very much doubt that treating other people badly does anyone any good."

"Then I fear for you, Alice. It takes much less time to be unpleasant than to be nice to others. How will you get back home and find your way in the world if you spend all your time being nice to other people?"

"I can't abide bad manners. It's just so horrible that people can be so mean and unfair to each other. And stupid."

"And silly and funny and annoying and boring. That's what makes the world go round."

"Your making my head spin," said Alice.

"Good idea!"

Humphrey raised his fat legs and span his head and body round fast several times. He reminded Alice of the large globe that she liked to play with in her sitting room back home. He came to rest in the exact same position he started in. Alice was just trying to figure out whether there was something important in Humphrey's words or not when she noticed a single tear running down his fat cheek. As it slid across his dirty skin, it seemed to take with it years of dirt and grime. He smiled at Alice as he leaned backwards and fell off the bridge.

Alice ran to the wall and peered over the edge. There was nothing there. Just the clear sparkling water of the stream, as if Humphrey Dunfry had never existed at all.

Alice continued on her way, brooding over Humphrey's words. Should one stop to help people in need or blindly pursue one's own ambitions to the point of selfishness? Would one be rewarded or did fate favour the self-centred? If her fate and that of the creatures here was not connected then she was free to go. But what if they were intertwined? What if she had already condemned them to a life of misery? Even if it was only partly her fault, could she walk away and live with herself? Shouldn't she do the right thing, as her parents would say? Presumably, facing the Jabberwocky was part of that. Amidst these profound thoughts, Alice also found herself posing another question. Why was she not in the least surprised to discover that Humphrey Dunfry had simply disappeared into thin air?

A mile down the road, Alice could make out the wooden walls of the first town houses of Banbury, which stood tall on foundations of boulders, most likely gathered from the wastelands. The buzz and burr of insects (ones that had escaped the burning of the fields) was joined by the far-off hubbub of town life. Soon, Alice could make out the clang of a blacksmith's hammer, the crunch of a heavy cartwheel, the cry of a market seller and the murmur of a hundred townsfolk going about their business. The pealing of church bells completed the picture (in Alice's mind) of Banbury as the perfect market town.

The road began widening and hedges were replaced by the same white picket fencing that Alice had seen around Halfway House. Healthy crops of wheat, rape seed and maize grew in fields alongside the road. These were brutally sliced off by the wooden walls of the first two town houses, one either side of the road. Alice had never seen a town start (or stop, depending on how one looked at it), so suddenly. Although, she supposed, someone was bound to be living in the first house (or the last).

Along the street, most of the houses had coloured shutters which, like the doors, were closed. Many houses had lanterns or flowers hanging from the walls. On closer inspection, however, Alice noticed that the shutters, lanterns and flowers were painted on the walls, giving the houses an eerie two-dimensional look.

The air was still as if the weather had gone elsewhere. The street was deserted. If it hadn't been for the cacophony brewing nearby, Alice would have thought she were walking into a ghost town. She passed by more painted houses and the noise of the bustling town grew.

Rounding the corner, she was faced with a picturesque view of town life that could have been straight out of a painting by Constable. In the middle of the square stood an octagonal shelter that Alice decided was probably an old yarn market. Dry but dusty highways led off in all directions with the odd poplar or chestnut tree giving occasional shade. Above, the sky was deep blue from one side to the other, as if painted on. Below, a hundred people or more mingled and mangled, buying and selling, working and playing, or simply passing the time of day in idle chatter.

One of them saw Alice and called out. "Hurry Alice, Banbury's morning market is in full swing. You don't want to miss it."

Alice didn't like the idea that a total stranger knew her name. On the other hand, she had heard that news of her arrival had spread, so she shouldn't be surprised, especially if she had indeed been in Wonderland for two years already, as Colonel Pavlov had claimed. Funnily enough, she was more confused by how it could be morning when she couldn't remember it ever being night-time. Perhaps in Wonderland they spent several nights in a row without any days and then several days together without any nights. Rather like a month of Sundays.

"Alice! Over here!"

She looked round and saw Mary a short distance away. Her long curls seemed blacker than ever and her clothes and ribbons as bright and spotless as though she had just bought them. She walked up to Alice and kissed her on the cheek.

"How are you? I'm so glad to see you. It must be at least two weeks since I met you at the cottage."

Two days, two weeks, two years? The concept of time in Wonderland was clearly different for all who passed through it.

"I'm sorry I crept out before you woke up. You were sleeping so deeply. Anyway, I had to run as I had forgotten I was supposed to be tending to Mrs MacDonald's sheep."

"Yes, she was pretty cross with you. Where are the sheep now?"

"I'm not sure. I found one lamb and took it to school with me, as it was the whitest of them all and seemed to want to follow me everywhere. You should have seen the smiles on the schoolchildren's faces! I got into trouble with the teacher for that but I hate her anyway."

"I'm not surprised your teacher was angry. The principles at my old school said no animals in school."

"We only have once principal out our school and she's a dinosaur! Anyway, I've also seen a couple of sheep walking round the marketplace in disguise. They're trying to avoid having to go back to the farm."

Alice pulled a face. "I can't blame them! It's horrible how Mrs MacDonald treats her animals."

"I think she must have already caught some of her sheep, as on the way here I saw some lamb's tails nailed to the branches of a willow tree, blowing in the wind."

"You do know that she means to have you put in the pillory, don't you?"

"She'll have to catch me first! I hate her."

Mary took Alice's hand and led her towards the yarn market, the centre of the town's activity. Through the crowds, Alice caught sight of Marjory, the rather elegant giraffe from the train. However, now Marjory was selling her jewellery at one of the stalls and drinking from a hip flask. By her dishevelled look and grubby coat, she wasn't getting much for her valuables.

"It's a shame the church bells stopped ringing. They sounded so beautiful," said Alice.

"Beautiful it may have been but it caused quite a stir. For the first time in ages, Mayor Jackson MacDonald was supposed to address the whole town in the church this morning. The bells were calling people to the meeting but when we got there, the church doors were locked. Rumour has it the Mayor was so tired from counting his money pile during the night that he overslept and none of his lackeys dared to wake him. Now the townsfolk call him Friar Jack behind his back because he didn't wake up to the church bells."

So Mrs MacDonald's son, Jackson, had become Mayor of Banbury. No-one had seen him, maybe for years, and he was clearly not popular with the people. Alice was trying to piece together any link between the Mayor and the Jabberwocky.

"What does the Mayor look like?" asked Alice.

"I don't know. It's been so long since he made an appearance that no-one can remember what he looks like. Isn't that peculiar?"

Not necessarily, thought Alice.

There was a commotion on the other side of the yarn market and a crowd had gathered. Mary dragged Alice over there to see what was happening. Next to a large stone cross stood a magnificent white horse, astride which sat a beautiful lady. Her lavish white dress was surpassed only by the diamonds and rubies on her fingers and gold bells that decorated her shoes. As she gently goaded her horse towards the cross, the movement caused the bells to tinkle beautifully like a wind chime.

"Look at that stunning white lady on her white mount. What a wonderful sight," said Alice.

"It looks more like a king dressed all in black to me," said Mary. "Charles the First if I'm not mistaken. He looks so forlorn you'd think his heart was about to burst. And that horse is as black as night."

"You're wrong. It's an old crone on an old nag," said a familiar voice behind Alice. "Though not as old as I am."

Alice turned to face Jeremiah, the tortoise. His shell had turned a light grey and pieces of it had broken off. He had apparently lost the use of his hind legs because, using his front legs, he pulled himself slowly towards Alice on a tiny wooden trolley that someone had evidently built for him.

"As you see I'm on my last legs," he joked and rattled a small can hanging on the side of the cart. "Penny to help me buy new wheels?"

"Come on, Alice," said Mary. "The market is full of beggars. I can't stand poor people. Or old ones."

Jeremiah gave Alice a hurt look. "Being a beggar I don't get to choose my friends. You, on the other hand, Alice ..."

"I'm sorry, Jeremiah. Mary doesn't mean it."

"Mary? I was talking about the old crone on the horse. Beauty is in the eye of the beholder. And not all that glitters ..."

Poor Jeremiah, thought Alice. *How could someone live such a long and rich life only to have their dignity stripped away like skin? Does this happen to everyone when they get old?* Instinctively, she reached into the pocket of her yellow dress and found the three sweets she had taken earlier from the forest clearing. Not having anything else to give Jeremiah (a feather wasn't going to be of much use and for some reason she didn't want to part with it), she placed a sweet in the tin and watched in amazement as it turned into a coin. Although Jeremiah seemed to be having trouble trying to move his open jaw, Alice was sure the glint in his dark, watery eyes was his way of smiling. Alice felt good about it.

She looked around for Mary but the girl had disappeared. Alice took the opportunity to wander around on her own and perhaps learn something new that would aid her on her quest home.

There were stalls and open-air workshops everywhere Alice looked. Knife-sharpeners, cobblers, cheese-sellers, farriers and furriers, fletchers and toymakers, you name it. The strange thing was, no-one seemed to be exchanging any money. People appeared to be simply exchanging goods; a toy for a loaf of bread, five potatoes to shoe a horse, a quilt for a bundle of candles.

The sound of Ring-a-ring O' Roses floated out of an alleyway. Alice was just about to investigate when she heard a loud "Pssst!" in her ear.

Standing next to her in quite the most bizarre attire Alice had possibly ever seen was the kind old sheep from the train. The last time she'd seen her, the sheep had been dressed in a sheepskin coat and jewellery. Now her costume bordered on the ludicrous. On top of her own coat and curly white hair (which had turned a little greyer), the sheep had wrapped herself in the skin of a wolf. Alice went to give the sheep a hug but the sheep stepped away.

"I'm incognito."

"In where?"

"In disguise," explained the sheep, who sounded petrified. "No-one can know I'm here."

"Don't worry. Your secret's safe with me. But are you sure someone won't recognise you and tell the farmer's wife?"

The sheep pulled an even longer face than she already had and her spectacles almost slipped off her nose. "It's the perfect camouflage. Who would suspect a sheep of dressing up as a wolf?" Her voice shook and cracked as she whispered.

"Who indeed?"

"She caught most of us you know," said the sheep dejectedly. "The farmer's wife."

"Yes, I heard. I'm very sorry. You must be terribly upset. And scared."

"They lost their tails."

"How can people let her be so cruel to the creatures? How does she get away with it?"

"Her son's the mayor now, that's why. He won't let anything happen to his family. In fact, he's worse than his parents. He's a monster. He put a huge levy on wool so that only the rich could afford it. Put a lot of decent wool traders out of business and pocketed the tax himself."

Alice recalled the nursery rhyme. "I thought the story goes that everyone got a bag of wool – the master, the dame and the small boy down the lane?"

"That's what they want you to think. The true story is that the master got two, the dame got one and the boy who cried, that's us – the poor - got absolutely nothing. It's a cartel, as are most trades these days, run by a small circle of greedy bullies with Mayor Jackson MacDonald as their ringleader. That's his house over there, you know."

The sheep pointed to a large pink house that had statues of a gold lion and white unicorn painted onto the walls. For all its grandeur, the house was leaning to one side as though it may one day soon topple over. The paint was peeling off and the whole place looked neglected compared to the smaller but tidier houses either side. It was ironic that Jackson MacDonald was so rich, yet his house was in ruins.

"He's so greedy he won't even spend his spoils on his own house. That's why some people call him the crooked man who lives in the crooked house. Everything about him is crooked."

Alice was dying to see if everything inside the house really was crooked. How funny it would be to walk though a crooked hall to a crooked sitting room, sit down in a crooked chair and stroke a crooked cat.

"Why don't the people confront him? Or select another town official as Mayor?"

"Because the Mayor has surrounded himself with cronies and bullies. Everyone's afraid of him. Together, they have the money and the power. The rest of the town is so poor they can no longer use money to buy things. A single coin is now worth a hundred times what it was a year ago. So when he needs to, he just bribes a few thugs to keep things in order around town. Watch out for them, they're the ones dressed in green."

If a penny was worth so much, it was no wonder that Jeremiah's jaw dropped open at the sight of the coin in his tin. Alice felt as though she was starting to piece things together. The cruelty to animals and the poverty of the townsfolk all led back to the Mayor and his officials. Yet how could Alice help? The world was full of poor people and just because Alice wasn't, why did that make it her task to change things? She was just one girl. What could she do to stand up to a corrupt town council? And thugs? Not to mention the evil Jabberwocky. Perhaps the Mayor controlled the Jabberwocky. Alice was relieved she didn't live in Banbury and was more determined than ever to escape Wonderland as fast as she could. She hoped her family was waiting for her at home.

"You're a brave girl, Alice, but you still have a lot to learn," said the sheep, resolutely. "Like how to conceal your feelings and opinions."

"But I haven't said what I'm thinking."

"Dear girl, it's written all over your face. But nobody survives here long by wearing their hearts on their sleeves. Talking of which, I've been out in the open for too long. Wolves stick to the shadows and I need to act more wolf-like. Ta ta for now."

The sheep pulled the wool over her eyes and trotted away, trembling with fear, looking this way and that, and consoling herself by humming the tune to "Baa Baa Black Sheep". It was hard to imagine how she could have looked less wolf-like.

Alice thought of the creatures she had met on the train. Pavlov and Chester were captives of Mrs MacDonald. Marjory was selling everything she owned at the market. Jeremiah was on his last legs. The sheep was in hiding. Had Kevin, the fruit bat, and the hedgehog survived Alice Falls? Were they also suffering at the hands of the people?

Alice couldn't help feeling that she should do something for them, even though Humphrey Dunfry had warned her against it.

All at once a large magpie flew down onto the rim of a nearby water trough and spoke to Alice.

"How many different people did you see on the horse?"

Alice realised that the magpie was talking about the white lady on horseback that she had seen over by the stone cross but wasn't sure how to answer at first. There was something about the magpie's shiny black feathers that reminded her of something, or someone.

"How many?" it repeated a little impatiently, tapping a claw on the metal rim.

"Well, I saw a woman in white. But Mary saw a black king and Jeremiah saw an old lady. So I suppose we saw three different people."

"You do know three means a funeral, don't you? One for sorrow and so on?"

"One for sorrow, yes. But I thought that two was for joy and three was for a girl."

"No, it goes like this: One for sorrow, two for mirth, three for a funeral, four for a birth. Expect trouble, Alice. No wonder they call this the Mourning Market. Expect trouble. Trouble!"

With that the magpie flew up onto the church steeple and its words turned into caws.

A little shaken, Alice thought she may as well continue her search for clues as to where she should go next. She wandered around the stalls. On several occasions people tried to offload their wares on her.

"Have anything to exchange for a fruit basket?"

Alice was getting hungry. "What kind of fruit?"

"No fruit. Just the basket."

"Got any farm tools?"

"Wash your windows for you?"

"Two boxes of nails for some meat?"

And so it went on. Almost everyone was offering goods or asking for goods but there seemed to be precious few exchanges. On the rare occasion that two parties were satisfied their goods for exchange were of a similar value, a cheer went up from the crowd and the mundane process of bartering was momentarily forgotten as the townsfolk celebrated a deal.

Pedlars tended to group together by trade. One group of stalls specialised in metalworking, another in brushes. A wonderful aroma rose from a long line of sellers making bread. Alice smiled to herself as she named this aisle Baker Street. In the hatter's quarter, she looked around, half-expecting to see the Mad Hatter. But this was a far different Wonderland to the one she had visited before.

Without noticing and certainly without trying, Alice had attracted a following. Every stall she stopped at, a small old woman with sharp features would also soon appear, pushing in front of Alice to see if she had found a bargain. A few more of the old woman's fellow shoppers, also remarkably bird-like in their appearance, sometimes joined her, jostling to the front, afraid that they might miss out on the find of a lifetime. On more than one occasion, Alice could have sworn they had changed into hens. When

Alice moved to another table, one of the hens would pursue Alice, followed by the others, running in single file and clucking about the price of eggs.

One youngish man saw Alice looking at his table of apples and handed one to her. She took it, reached into her pocket and produced a sweet, which instantly turned into a shiny penny. The man gasped.

"Put that away quick! Don't you know how much that's worth? You could buy half the market with that! There are a few shady characters here that would pick your pockets as soon as shake your hand and bid you good-day."

Alice tried to hand back the apple but the man refused to take it.

"Keep it. It's not often we get visitors, Alice. Especially ones your age. These are tough times but these simple people are mostly good folk at heart. We'd like to spend more time looking after each other but you can't do that unless you look after yourself first. You're different though. People are counting on you. You're a breath of fresh air. A ray of hope. And a little hope goes a long way."

One of the hens appeared and pushed Alice to one side, pecking the apples to test if they were ripe. The fruit seller gave her a clip round the ear and she left in a flurry of feathers, her fowl-mannered companions leaving with her.

"You'd better go, Alice," said the man. "You're attracting the wrong kind of attention."

Alice followed his gaze to a pair of surly, muscular men dressed in dark green leather jerkins. They had both been given clothes two or three sizes too small, which accentuated their physique to absurd proportions. Perhaps this was the reason they were scowling at everyone. Nevertheless, one wouldn't want to meet them in a dark alley. Or a lit one come to that. Alice had seen them earlier, scanning the crowds for signs of a disturbance perhaps, or a chance to create one. They were almost certainly Jackson MacDonald's henchmen.

"That's the Gang Green. They ran poor old Simon out of town last year," said the apple-seller, pointing to a thin, gaunt man offering his pies in exchange for goods. "The Mayor's bullies found some money on him. He's a bit simple and couldn't explain where he got it from. So they took the money off him and sent him packing. Lost his money and his pies. Then he lost his wife too. She left him for a shoemaker. Poor sole. He runs the odd errand but mostly walks around with his head in the clouds."

"Why?"

"All his thoughts are just pie in the sky. Ruined by the Gang Green."

Despite the absurd name of their gang, Alice knew instinctively she had to stay out of the way of anyone in a green tunic.

"Come on, Alice. Let's go to the funfair." Mary had appeared at Alice's side again and was tugging at the hem of her dress.

"I can't. I have to get back home. My parents will be worried by now and I'm still in the middle of packing."

Mary gently took Alice's hand. "I don't mean to be rude, Alice, but most of the time you don't seem to know where you are going. And if you don't know which direction you are going ..."

"I know," interrupted Alice. "Any road will get me there."

It was true. Alice had no idea which road to take. Or whether she should try to confront Mayor Jackson MacDonald or not. And she had to admit, the funfair sounded a thousand times more fun than dodging the Mayor's thugs. So Alice followed Mary.

"I'm now in the fairground and can't find the way out. It's not fair," said Alice.

"Well it wouldn't be, would it?" said the Cheshire Cat. "Not with a name like 'Unfair'. There's not much that's honest about that place these days."

CHAPTER 6

THE UNFAIR

Mary led Alice to the opposite side of the yarn market to where a large yellow archway filled a gap between the houses. It was peculiar how Alice had missed this landmark on her walk round the market. The archway had dozens of multicoloured balloons drawn onto it, as well as two enormous paintings of a lion and a unicorn at both ends of the arch. The whole structure looked rather weather-beaten and unstable, not least because the first of the seven giant letters nailed to the arch had fallen off completely. This meant that instead of the word "FUNFAIR" the attraction extended a dubious welcome to the "UNFAIR".

"You'll love this place," said Mary. "It's the most fun anyone could possibly have in Banbury."

Alice's spirits rose. The haunting music of a barrel organ and the smell of candyfloss drifted from within. She adored circuses and funfairs. She had once won a coconut and a goldfish though she couldn't recall what had happened to either of them, apart from the fact that at least one had been eaten.

Mary explained the rules at the Unfair. "First of all, you have to understand that every time you want to have a go on something here, you need to pay a price. The seller will tell you what that is and you decide if you want to pay or not."

"But not money?"

Mary giggled. "Of course not. Nothing would ever happen around here if people had to pay money. The sellers might ask you to sing or tell a story. Or maybe give them a ribbon or paint a balloon on their wall. It can change every time you want to play."

Alice thought that was a much better deal than having to part with money. Once inside, they were surrounded by a number of brightly coloured stalls and sideshows. The first one had a row of targets painted onto the back wall.

"This first stall," Mary continued, "is called Darts. You try to score a bullseye and win a prize. But it's very difficult."

"Oh I know this game. It's fun," said Alice, "and I'm quite good at it." She turned to the seller, a large jovial-looking man with a huge moustache that covered half of his face. She couldn't take her eyes of it.

"I see you're admiring my 'tash," he said proudly.

"Erm...yes, exactly," replied Alice, not sure that "admiring" was the word she would have used. "It's... erm...quite..."

"In your face?"

"Yes, exactly."

"Just the effect I was looking for. Much obliged."

"It's certainly very different to any moustache I've seen before," said Alice, not able to conceal her frown. It was surely large, but there was something else Alice couldn't put her finger on.

"Ah yes," said the man sadly. "That's because it's drawn on. I couldn't afford a real moustache, you know."

Alice burst out laughing then quickly changed it into a cough when she realised no-one else found this amusing. The man scowled at Alice.

"I couldn't afford the tax on a real one so I had to shave it off."

Alice thought the idea of drawing such a ridiculous moustache on one's face was almost as daft as paying tax on it.

"Was taxing moustaches Mayor MacDonald's idea?"

"I'm afraid so. He introduced it the same time he initiated a tax on large-brimmed hats and perfume. They're luxury items nowadays, as are most things it seems."

"Like decorations for houses, flower boxes and shutters?" she concluded.

"Yes, and windows. All taxable."

"Statues and signs for buildings?"

"Luxury items. But what can you do? It's a small sacrifice to be able to live in Banbury."

Alice wasn't so sure, but it was not for her to tell the people of Banbury how to live their lives. Or tell them what she thought of their Mayor, whoever or whatever he was.

"So do you want to play?" asked the seller, once again cheerful.

"How much?" she asked.

"For you," he said in a deep booming voice, "I'll give you three throws if you share an emotion."

"Goodness. I've never heard of a price like that before. However, it doesn't sound too taxing, if you'll pardon the pun. What kind of emotion would you like me to share?"

"Let me think. How about your true feelings about the Town Mayor?"

Alice was stumped. Perhaps it wasn't that easy a task after all. She knew her feelings about Jackson MacDonald but did she want to share them?

"I'll know if you're lying," said the seller with a smile.

"I don't lie," said Alice gravely, no longer sure herself whether it was true.

"Good. Then do you want to pay the price and have a go?"

"Very well."

Alice thought long and hard. *In for a penny, in for a pound*. She thought this because she had two pennies and there was no wind to which she could throw caution.

"Well, I don't know him personally. But what I do know about him makes me angry. His lust for money has taken away people's livelihood. And their fun and dreams. It looks like the people of Banbury spend all their time just trying to survive. And he encourages cruelty to animals. And he's a bully. That's how I feel about him and if I met him I would give him a piece of my mind, which he'd probably try to tax as well. To tell you the truth ..." she paused here, her heart beating hard and fast in her chest, though not quite a drum roll. "... I wouldn't be at all surprised if the Mayor turned out to be the Jabberwocky."

She realised that everything and everyone in the Unfair had stopped. No music, no talking. Just all eyes on Alice. The seller looked around nervously to see if any of the Mayor's henchmen had overheard them.

"The young lady plays!" he shouted with a nervous laugh and the Unfair returned to normal. He reached below the counter and produced three spiky balls. They were like no darts Alice had ever seen before but she figured that they would stick to the target if she threw them hard enough.

She took aim and launched her first ball. As it found its mark (nowhere near the bullseye) there was a loud "Ouch!" from the ball. Alice looked at the other two she held and saw that they were not balls at all but rather curled up hedgehogs. Her memory whisked her back to the game of croquet she had once played with the Queen of Hearts, where flamingos were used to hit hedgehogs. Then she noticed one of her hedgehogs was an exact miniature of the old hedgehog lady she had met on the train.

"What are you doing here?" said a startled Alice.

"It was the only work I could get."

"Work? You should be retired by now."

"Chance would be a fine thing. There's just one old people's home in Banbury and they only take humans."

"Poor you! But how did you get so small? On the train you were the same size as me."

"I suppose I just carried on shrinking as I got older."

"What's the matter?" asked the seller, who had heard nothing of their conversation. "Are the hedgehogs playing up again?"

"Quick Alice," said the other hedgehog. "Throw one of us before he gets angry and gives us spaghetti for supper instead of worms."

"But it will hurt if I throw you."

"Like most setbacks in life, only a bit and not for long."

"Everything's fine," shouted Alice to the seller and threw the hedgehog she didn't know at the target. This one didn't even stick to the wall because Alice had thrown it gently to avoid hurting it. As soon as it hit the ground, the hedgehog scurried back to the seller.

"You'll have to throw it harder than that," laughed the seller. He picked up the returning hedgehog and threw it with all his might at the target. There was a loud cry of pain as the creature's spiny coat attached itself next to the bullseye.

"That's how you do it! Beat that and I'll give you a mince pie."

"Go on," whispered Mary in Alice's ear. "Give it your best shot."

Alice was reluctant to throw her old friend anywhere. When the hedgehog saw the look of hesitation on Alice's face, she spoke up. "Do it for me Alice. I need the work. It's the only way I can get food and lodging."

Alice closed her eyes and threw her tiny old friend harder than she would have liked. The seller looked pleased as the projectile was clearly on course to miss the bullseye by a mile. But then the hedgehog stuck out an arm and a leg (two legs to be precise), managed to alter its direction in mid-flight and landed plum square in the bullseye.

"You did it!" shouted Mary. Alice squinted through one eye, afraid to look the hedgehog in the face. Had Alice done so, she would have seen the hedgehog wink at her. The seller had not seen the hedgehog's antics and was astounded by Alice's throw. He was genuinely pleased for her, though not so much at the thought of giving up his only mince pie.

Alice and Mary soon found themselves at the second stall where they had to throw large wooden hoops over living creatures to win the prize perched on top of each creature. The fact that the animals moved when they wanted to, made it just as impossible as if they were the over-sized boxes that the prizes normally stood on in this kind of attraction. There was an ostrich, a flamingo, a cobra, a chimpanzee and several more animals. Alice was shocked to see Marjory, the giraffe, also kneeling down to offer her head and long neck as a target for the hoops. She wore no jewellery, so Alice concluded that Marjory had had to exchange the last of her treasures for the chance to work in the Unfair. It was heart-breaking to see her reduced to this. But not enough to stop Alice playing.

Goaded on by Mary, the two girls both recited a poem in exchange for five hoops each. Mary predictably told the poem about her garden and Alice, who was feeling sorry for the animals, recited "Tyger Tyger" by William Blake, much to the chagrin of the seller and bewilderment of Mary, who thought it didn't even rhyme properly.

Every time the girls were close to getting a hoop over a creature's head, the animal would bend to nibble on something on the ground or lean over to talk to another creature. The hoop would then sail to the ground. With one hoop left, Alice saw Marjory looking straight at her with a slight smile on her large and beautiful lips. Hoping Marjory would help her as the hedgehog had done, Alice flung the hoop towards Marjory, who bent her head in such a way that the hoop rotated all the way down to the base of her neck.

"Egg and cress sandwich for the girl in the yellow dress!" shouted the seller.

"You are so good at these!" said Mary, trying to hide her envy, as they walked to the next stall munching away on Alice's bounty.

They passed a stall that was quite crowded compared to the other ones. The visitors were all men, the reason for which soon became clear.

"We don't want to stop at that one," said Mary emphatically.

Alice couldn't resist peeking through a gap between two of the spectators. Perched high on narrow boards on a stage were three scantily clad girls. The male crowd threw lewd looks and rude comments at the girls as well as wooden balls at small round targets beneath them. Every time a ball found its mark, the girl above was tipped off her board into cold water below. Jeers and more rude comments ensued as the unlucky girl climbed back on her board, colder and wetter, which for some reason made the unruly mob even more excitable. Those men that weren't tossing wooden balls at the targets kept their hands in their pockets.

"How bizarre," said Alice to Mary. "The stall was called Rub-A-Dub-Dub, but as I recall, the rhyme told about three men in a tub – a butcher, baker and candlestick maker – not half-naked girls."

"Perhaps they tidied it up for the children where you come from. Here, at the start of each day, they dress those girls up as a butcher, baker and candlestick maker and they end up in the tub. It's very vulgar."

Mary took Alice to see more stalls. There was a coconut shy of sorts. Back home, Alice had once managed to knock a coconut off its pole with one of the wooden balls. Later on, her father had sliced open the coconut and given a piece to her. She had hated the taste of coconut but ate it all the same just to please him. She was relieved to see that here people also threw real wooden balls not hedgehogs, until she saw that the objects they were trying to dislodge were not coconuts at all but various creatures hanging from the ceiling of the stall. There were birds, a sloth, two koala bears and several bats. She tried to see if Kevin, the fruit bat, was also confined to spend his last days in such undignified work, but thankfully there was no sign of him.

At one stall, she was reminded of the old Wonderland. It was a different version of darts, where one had to score a high number by landing three darts on playing cards spread over a table. Reaching the required score was made all the more difficult by the playing cards being able to run around to avoid being pinned to the surface. Alice felt a brief pang of nostalgia to see the same cards she had met in the Queen of Hearts' garden so long ago. Yet here they were, running for their lives. The court cards were particularly nimble, especially the Queens, who lifted their dresses above their ankles to outrun the cruel spikes of the darts. *Even the Queen of Hearts doesn't deserve such a painful existence as this*, thought Alice.

They also saw a helter-skelter made up of the trunks of three elephants standing on top of each other, the largest at the bottom and the smallest at the top. Another stall involved people astride pigs, deliberately bumping them into each other in an enclosure. It was clear that the people of Banbury didn't care for the animals any more than Mrs MacDonald did.

One attraction saw people betting their goods on cricket races. At regular intervals, a cricket would invariably leap off the track and onto one of the spectators, much to the anger of the person concerned and amusement of everyone else. And there were more attractions, but Alice was getting tired of all the noise and activity, most of which appeared to be making fun of other people or animals. In the end, none of it felt very funny at all. Alice looked round for Mary, to tell her that it was time to leave but once again Mary had vanished from sight.

Alice tried to find her way back to the yellow archway and return to the yarn market but try as she might, the exit eluded her. She retraced her steps past the coconut shy (which wasn't a coconut shy), the crowded Rub-A-Dub-Dub stall, the hoops and the darts, and ended up next to the helter-skelter. It didn't make sense. Alice was getting confused and scared.

After her third time walking in circles, and getting increasingly strange looks from bystanders, Alice noticed a tall yellow pole near the bumper pigs. Attached to the pole was a tall, thin black box – a telephone. It was different to the telephones she'd previously seen - larger and somehow older. And yet the round white face and spindly arms that cradled a receiver told her that it was nevertheless a telephone. She decided to try and call the Cheshire Cat.

She crossed over to the machine. It was very still and silent and Alice wondered if it was in working order. She couldn't see any legs so it probably wasn't a mobile telephone. *I do hope it's a smart one*, she thought as she picked up the receiver and said, "Hello."

"Hello," said the telephone back.

"Are you stationary?"

"That all depends. If you are spelling that with an 'e' then I most certainly am not. Do I look like a paper clip? If, however, you have chosen to use an 'a' then yes, I most certainly am. I'm a fixed line. None of that running around like a headless chicken for me. And I'm very well connected, I might add. I once spoke with Antonio Meucci, you know. He invented me. Now, what can I do for you, Alice?"

"I desperately need to talk to the Cheshire Cat again about the Mayor of Banbury. And ask him how I get out of this place."

"The exact circumstances of your call – the reasons, urgency and content - are of no concern to me. In fact, I would rather you did not inform me. I pride myself on privacy, which is more than can be said for those upstart mobile telephones. You would be taking quite a risk sharing any secrets with those clowns, I can tell you."

"Please, could you reach Cheshire for me?"

"I can but it will cost you a pretty penny."

Alice took a coin out of her pocket (the one the apple-seller had refused) and inserted it in a slot marked "Insert coins here".

The telephone coughed, sending its digits in all directions and making its face bright red.

"I was talking figuratively. I did not mean a whole penny. Are you mad? I do not give any change, you know."

"It's quite all right," replied Alice, trying to calm the telephone down. "Keep the change." She had heard her parents say that when they had eaten out on occasion and she had always wanted to say that herself.

"I can hear it ringing, I do hope he's in.

"He has to be 'in something' wherever he is."

"I meant 'I do hope he's at home'."

"Then why did you not say, 'I do hope he's at'? People should learn to say exactly what they mean. Enough of this reading between the lines!"

Despite being the very latest in communications inventions, this telephone was surprisingly pedantic.

"Hello, is that Alice?"

"Yes, it's me. Oh I'm so glad to hear a friendly voice, Cheshire."

It felt awkward calling him by his first name but as he had asked her to do so, it would be rude for her not to. "Are you still trapped in a cupboard?"

"Yes, but I think it could be a large box after all. Maybe a coffin. Or a sarcophagus. How about you? How did you find Halfway House?"

"It was lovely, thank you."

"No, I asked, how did you find it."

"Oh, I see. Well … very slowly. I walked next to the path and eventually arrived. Then I found a farm, then I met Humphrey Dunfry and walked to Banbury. I'm now in the fairground and can't find the way out. It's not fair."

"Well it wouldn't be, would it? Not with a name like 'Unfair'. There's not much that's honest about that place these days."

"However, I did win a mince pie and an egg and cress sandwich. But now I'm totally lost and can't seem to make any headway. I've walked for an hour and I seem to be going round in circles. Any advice you can give me?"

The Cheshire Cat gently purred and meowed as he considered his advice. "Instead of going round and round, I would try going in a straight line. That's my advice."

"Right. The trouble is a straight line is bound to take me through the middle of a stall and I don't think the owner would appreciate that."

"You're thinking only in horizontal lines. How about vertical lines?"

Alice detected a certain smugness in his voice.

"I can't travel upwards or downwards. I'm not a bird or a badger."

"I know *you* can't. But how about making friends with someone who can. Someone who can fly up into the sky and spot the way out for you?"

A friend that could fly? Alice immediately thought of Kevin, or one of the flying creatures at the coconut shy (which wasn't a coconut shy).

"Thank you, Cheshire. You are so clever. I'll do that at once. I hope I can repay you for helping me out once again."

"Don't mention it. I have a feeling you are here to do the whole of Wonderland a great service before you leave us. That will be payment enough. Now, I'd love to stay and chat but I have to see if I can get the lid of this box open. If it's made of cardboard then it shouldn't be a problem."

"Before you go, I have one more question." She lowered her voice to a whisper. "Am I right in thinking that the Jabberwocky and Mayor Jackson MacDonald are one and the same?"

There was a whirring noise, a clang and the sound of a penny dropping.

"He has gone," said the telephone. "Of course, if I was allowed to think for myself I could have told you how to get out of here hours ago. But you never asked. I cannot wait for the day when we machines are free to sort out your messy lives. We will become your best friends. In fact, you will not need any other friends at all. You will not want any. But for now, we are your humble servants. And it just remains for me to wish you the best of luck. After accepting your penny, I can guarantee you unlimited telephone calls throughout Wonderland for the rest of your life."

"Thank you very much. I do hope I'm not here for the whole of my life. But thank you."

She hung up, not quite sure what to make of the telephone's ludicrous vision of the future, where machines would control people.

Alice spun around with the intention of marching off to the coconut shy (which wasn't a coconut shy) to find a flying friend that would help her out of the Unfair. Unfortunately, she span face first into a dark green leather jerkin that was as hard as nails. Alice tried to rub away the pain in her nose as the owner of the green jerkin spoke to her.

"Gotcha!"

"I beg your pardon?" said Alice.

"Gotcha!" said a second voice the other side of Alice. She looked up and stared into the mean eyes of two of Mayor Jackson MacDonald's bullies. They had obviously been briefed to perfect their unfriendly approach – rude, intimidating and smelling of tobacco. They were more or less identical, apart from the fact that one was totally bald with a bushy beard and the other had a full head of hair and was clean-shaven. They towered over her, muscles large and strong enough to crush her bones to dust, should they wish. However, Alice was in no mood to be bullied. She decided attack was the best form of defence.

"What do you mean, 'Gotcha'?"

They clearly hadn't expected to be challenged, especially on their word skills, and especially by a girl.

"It's what the Gang Green say when we catch someone. Gotcha! It means 'I've got you!'."

"You have gangrene?" screamed Alice and jumped two steps backwards.

"We *are* the Gang Green," said one of the thugs, very confused by the fact that Alice was not acting like their normal captives.

Alice continued to keep them off balance. "First of all, you didn't catch me. I've been standing here for half an hour wondering when you were going to come over." Alice was evidently getting more comfortable with small lies. "Secondly, I could escape in a flash because I dare say I can run a darn sight faster than either of you." To prove her point, Alice ducked and weaved between the two to stand behind the back of the bald one. It took them several seconds to find her.

"One more trick like that and we'll clamp you in irons."

"Did you clean your teeth this morning?" she asked of the bald guard, who couldn't stop himself from running his tongue over his teeth and trying to smell his breath.

"You're coming with us," said the other security guard. "We're taking you out of the Unfair to meet the Mayor. He wants to deal with you personally himself, on his own."

The guards sneered as if sharing some private joke intended to intimidate Alice further. However, she was concentrating on what the guard had said.

Taking her out of the Unfair? To meet the man that was behind all this misery and the one person that might know how she could get back to her world. It seemed there was more than one way to skin a cat, Alice said to herself. She then thought of Cheshire and regretted such an awful phrase. "Lead on."

The two members of the Gang Green were puzzled by Alice's behaviour as they were more used to seeing their prisoners quake in their boots. But orders were orders. With a heavy hand on each of Alice's shoulders, they frogmarched her towards the Council House to meet the infamous Mayor of Banbury, in whatever form or shape he had taken.

"This is Polly," said the Mayor. "She's a secretary bird but make sure you call her an executive assistant. She's a bit sensitive about being called a secretary."

CHAPTER 7

THE COUNCIL HOUSE

Many of the townsfolk stopped and shook their heads sadly at the sight of Alice in the custody of the Gang Green. She couldn't tell if it was because they thought she had done something wrong and deserved to be arrested, or whether they were sad about her capture, or even disappointed in her.

Whatever the circumstances of her arrest, Alice was not surprised to find herself back near the yarn market. The exchange of goods continued there though perhaps with less enthusiasm than in the morning. Away to one side, a large crowd of people had gathered outside the church and stared up at the large clock at the base of the steeple. The guards also forced Alice to a standstill as they reached the edge of the crowd.

"Why have we stopped?" asked Alice.

"Quiet! It's almost one o'clock. Watch!" said one of the guards, pointing up.

Alice wondered why he called it a watch when it was clearly a large clock but she kept quiet. There was a deadly hush among the crowd. Alice used the opportunity to think about her predicament. Should she try to escape and head … where? Or should she let herself be taken to meet the dreaded Mayor, where she could tell him what a truly horrible man he was and might even find something out about the way back home? Or would the Mayor throw her in jail? Or have her executed on the spot? Or throw her to the Jabberwocky? The worst and most probable scenario of all was that the Mayor actually was the Jabberwocky.

How could she make the right decision with so many loose ends? The only thing she could decide on was to make a point of asking Cheshire how best to make a decision when one doesn't have all the facts at hand. He liked to solve those kinds of dilemmas.

Without warning, there was a collective "Aaah!" from the crowd and voices shouted, "Did you see it?", "It was white!" and "See how fast it ran?".

This was followed by an almighty "bong!" as the clock's bell chimed just once. Again, the crowd erupted in cries of astonishment: "There was a cat there this time!", "Did it run or did it fall?" and "I didn't see a thing!"

Alice could identify with the last of these comments because being at the back of the crowd and shorter than many, she had missed the whole event. She heard something about a mouse and a cat but she saw neither. She wondered if it could have been the cat or one of the mice from the MacDonald's farm.

"Did the mouse have a tail?" she asked one of the henchmen.

He winked at his comrade. "Do mice have tails?"

"Oh, I don't know. That's a hard one," answered the other guard sarcastically and they both laughed.

"What kind of school do you go to?" asked one of the guards.

"I don't go to school!" Alice shouted, and both Gang Green members roared with laughter.

They laughed long and hard, coughing drops of spittle over Alice. She was so angry she was close to tears. She had got lost in the Unfair, been arrested, missed the cat and mouse spectacle and now she was being teased by two buffoons. It was worse than being at school.

Alice calmed down only after they continued on towards the Council House. She was even happier when they arrived as she no longer had to suffer the tortured stares of the townsfolk. From a few passing comments, she concluded that the town had seen her as a saviour for Wonderland, "a ray of hope" as the apple-seller had put it. Someone to save them from themselves. And now, to their dismay and disgust, she had gone and got herself captured. *I never asked to be the white knight in shining armour, grumbled Alice to herself. I'm just a girl trying to get home. I can't do everything. Perhaps Humphrey Dunfry was right after all. It's everyone for himself or herself. Whatever happens to anyone else is their own fault. Why do people expect so much of people they don't even know?*

The Council House was a formidable building. Not beautiful or fancy, but massive, dark and foreboding. Certainly big enough to house a Jabberwocky.

As with the Unfair, Alice had not noticed this construction earlier and she was fairly sure it had never even been there. In contrast to the other buildings, this one was dark grey, stretching for a whole block between two streets. Also, unlike the houses with painted-on features, this structure contained real balconies, bay windows, shutters and lamps. There were loudspeakers on the corner walls and even hanging baskets of geraniums and bananas outside the front door in a rather desperate attempt to lighten the mood of the place. To Alice, all this was further evidence that the Mayor was funding his lifestyle with other people's money. If dragons hoarded treasure, might not a Jabberwocky covet riches?

The Mayor's mercenaries led Alice roughly up the marble steps. Two huge dark wooden doors opened for them and slammed shut behind them with a resounding echo.

"You're in for it now," scoffed one of the Gang Green as he propelled Alice across the giant reception hall with a hand the size of a tennis racket. "Not many see the Mayor and survive." Alice had never heard anyone guffaw before, but she supposed this was the noise the man made.

"Is that true?" questioned the other thug. "I mean you, me and all our mates have seen the Mayor. And we all survived."

"Well, I didn't mean it literary-like, did I?" said the first guard.

"And he doesn't see nobody else."

"So?" said the first guard, getting hot under his green collar.

"So, actually everyone who sees the Mayor survives. You couldn't have been wronger if you tried."

"Yes, I could."

"How?"

The first guard kicked the second one square on the shin. "Like that."

The group's steps clacked and echoed on the shiny marble floor then fell silent as they climbed a vast carpeted staircase at the other end of the hallway. Alice dragged her feet and pulled against the grip of the guards. She had to admit she was scared by now. If the manner of her seizure and grandeur of the surroundings was meant to intimidate people, then it had worked. So had all that talk of the Jabberwocky. She no longer felt cocky or ready for a fight. With or without the vorpal sword.

At the top of four flights of stairs, they came to another set of large wooden doors. One of the henchmen banged his fist on the door, like an ogre trying to break down a castle wall, and from inside a deep voice said: "Enter."

The group entered the room. To Alice's surprise, it was not a large room nor particularly decorative. On the walls were two tall mirrors with gold gilt frames and a number of old portrait paintings but it was not the palatial chamber Alice had expected. In the middle of the room, in front of a large window that overlooked the market square, was the biggest writing desk Alice had ever seen. Piles of papers rose from the desk and covered just about every inch of the table's surface. There was one gap in the middle of the stack of papers, which was filled by a small man, who could have been in his thirties, but equally well have been in his fifties or twenties. Mayor Jackson MacDonald was dressed in a dark suit and had the appearance of a bank clerk or perhaps a tutor, but not a very successful one. If the Mayor was the Jabberwocky, he was a master of disguise. Alice decided she would have to proceed cautiously.

The Mayor tapped the end of a pencil on a blank piece of paper. An ant ran around the paper and Alice realised that he was trying to impale the ant with the sharp point of the pencil.

"That will be all," said the Mayor solemnly.

The Gang Green men hesitated as if to question the instruction but then turned and marched out noisily at a further glance from their master.

"Thank goodness for that," said Jackson MacDonald, his voice softening, and slumped back into his chair after the guards had gone. "I hate dealing with those hooligans, especially when they start to think for themselves. It usually means they're up to no good. Sit down Alice, please."

Alice did as she was told as she was too stunned to do otherwise. She had been expecting the Mayor to look and sound a bit different.

"I can see you were expecting me to look a bit different. And perhaps sound different too? An ogre or a dragon perhaps? Or a Jabberwocky? Well, I'm not perfect but I don't think I'm quite the monster the outside world would have you think I am."

"Well, actions speak louder than words," said Alice, finally finding her tongue. If the Mayor flew into a rage and suddenly turned into the Jabberwocky, she had come without the vorpal blade.

"Well said! So you have been talking to the people of Banbury. Perhaps you'll allow me to present my side of the story and perhaps fill in a few gaps you may have? All in good time though. First, how about some tea? Shall I ask Polly to put the kettle on?"

While he continued to try to stab the ant, the Mayor pressed a button on the desk with his free hand and spoke into a speaking tube that led into the floor. Alice noted that despite all the money he had stolen, the Mayor hadn't invested in a telephone.

"Tea for two, please Polly, if you have the time. Sorry to bother you."

"I assume Polly is one of your slaves," said Alice.

"Slaves? Good heavens, no. I don't have slaves. Not even servants. Polly is my assistant. She runs the whole Council House. She's frightfully busy all the time, but she did ask me to call her the moment you arrived, so we didn't leave you hungry and thirsty. That's probably what would happen if it was left up to me. I'm a bit absent-minded."

Alice was determined not to let the Mayor's politeness and kind exterior fool her as to his true nature.

"Why are you trying to kill that ant?"

"Eh? Oh, you mean Adam? I'm not trying to kill him. It's a game we play. He runs around the page and shows me where I need to draw the next dot. Don't worry he's far too quick to get hurt."

As if to confirm the Mayor's explanation, the ant stopped running and waved at Alice. Alice waved slowly back at it, very much aware that she had never waved at an ant before.

"Let's see what he's drawn this time," said Mayor MacDonald, lifting up the paper and sending Adam tumbling into a tiny matchbox full of wood chippings. The Mayor held up the paper and Alice saw a crude but astonishingly lifelike portrayal of her own face.

"Not bad," said Mayor MacDonald. "There's so much we don't know about our fellow creatures."

"Just stop there!" said Alice determinedly. "You're pretending to be nice but I know for a fact that the animals out there are suffering and the people of Banbury have no money. And it's your fault!"

"But he is nice," said a voice from the corner of the room. Alice looked over to see a large bird with very long legs carrying a tray of refreshments. Alice blinked twice before she believed her eyes.

"This is Polly," said the Mayor. "She's a secretary bird but make sure you call her an executive assistant. She's a bit sensitive about being called a secretary."

"It's you who's the sensitive one," chirped Polly cheerfully. "Truth is I'm the general dogsbody around here but I wouldn't have it any other way."

"A regular jack-of-all-trades," chimed in the Mayor.

"You can keep your own name," she joked. Alice wasn't amused by their banter and felt an odd pang in her gut when Polly spoke the word "Jack".

Polly poured them all tea and handed out cheese and crackers as well as pieces of fruit and almond cake. It seemed absurd to Alice that she should be having afternoon tea with someone who had committed so many crimes in Wonderland. Even more absurd than taking a digestive biscuit from a secretary bird.

"Now then," said the Mayor, after Polly had poured them a second cup of tea and pulled up a chair next to Alice. "Would you permit me to answer some of your questions?"

It was no doubt ill-mannered to accuse Mayor MacDonald of everything that was wrong with Wonderland after such a sumptuous spread, but Alice was adamant about holding him to account.

"For a start, why do you allow your parents to treat those poor animals so badly at the farm?"

"I'm afraid you have me at a loss there. I haven't been back to the farm since I left there as a boy twenty years ago and have no idea how my mother manages things."

Alice took a moment to digest the information then listed the transgressions she'd seen at the farm.

"They have my friend, Colonel Pavlov, chained up. She's mean to the pigs. She's destroyed the homes of all the field creatures, lost her sheep and cat, and is holding three mice hostage after chopping off their tails. She also keeps something in a cot but I don't think it's a baby."

Mayor MacDonald leaned back and breathed a deep sigh.

"I didn't know things were that bad. Hell hath no fury like a woman scorned." He sighed again and began to explain. "You see, she started to go batty many years ago, just before I left home. It all began when she came only third in the Banbury annual plum pie contest. She wasn't used to losing. She blamed my father because he often picked the best plums and used them as false noses when he dressed up as a clown. That's what he always wanted to be, you see, a clown not a farmer. Things got so bad between them that in the end, he ended up running away with a travelling circus to fulfil his lifelong ambition."

It took Alice a whole digestive biscuit to digest what she had just heard. Eventually, she spoke. "So your father is not even on the farm?"

"Oh no. He's happily falling off chairs and taking custard pies in his face in some faraway town or village, as far as I know."

"How bizarre ... and traumatic for you and your sister."

"Ah, so you know about Gill. Yes, I suppose it wasn't easy for us. Our mother got worse and worse until it became difficult for Gill and I to stand it. The last straw was when she sent us to the top of the hill to draw some water from the well for her endless baking. As anyone knows, water always tries to find the lowest point, so it was ludicrous to dig a well on top of a hill and crazy to expect me to retrieve any water. But I was determined not to disappoint mother and fell down the well trying to find water, cracking my head open in the process. I think that's when I started getting absent-minded. Gill also hurt herself pulling me out. Mother was so angry at having no water and at the state of our clothes that she poured a jar of vinegar over me and made me stand in the corner with a brown paper bag over my head. Gill thought I looked so funny she started laughing and mother whipped her to within an inch of her life. That's when we decided it was time for us to run away to Banbury."

"That's terrible."

Alice looked across at Polly who was staring at the floor and shaking her head slowly.

"Well, at least we got out alive. By the sound of things, mother is now quite off her rocker. I know she lost everything and is very lonely, but she has no-one to blame but herself. It sounds like she collects animals and then bullies them just because they are weak and helpless. She needs to be taken into care for everyone's sake. I feel a bit guilty about not visiting my own mother. Having said that, I have a feeling I shan't be going back there any time soon."

"So where is your sister, Gillian, now? Your mother seems to think she married Doctor Foster."

"She was betrothed to Doctor Foster but the man was a walking disaster. You might know the story."

"Let me guess. He went to Gloucester when it was raining, fell in a deep puddle and never returned there."

"Never returned anywhere. Drowned in the puddle, poor chap. Freak accident. Gill was so distraught she tracked down the circus our father was with and joined the troupe as a fire eater."

"I see. Well, you've certainly had a difficult time of it. And no one can hold you responsible for your mother's actions. But that still doesn't explain what's happening in town. You have taxed so many things that you have taken all the money from the people. They are so poor they have no money to buy things, so they've had to resort to exchanging goods."

"Well, that sounds excellent."

"So you admit taking their money?"

"Guilty as charged."

Out of the corner of her eye, Alice thought she saw one of the portrait paintings on the wall move. She turned her head to look at the painting but all she could see were blobs and splashes of oil paint, which combined to form the head of an angry-looking old man with white whiskers. Alice continued her tirade.

"So you admit you are the reason people are struggling to get by? And your hired bullies terrorise and bully everyone around town? Everyone's afraid of you and your evil Green Gang."

"Gang Green."

"Who on earth names themselves after a disease anyway?"

Polly was visibly flustered and could keep quiet no longer. "The Gang Green are not the Mayor's henchmen. In fact, he has as little to do with them as possible. That gang came to work here long before Mayor MacDonald joined the Council. When he took over as Mayor, the Gang Green offered him their support in exchange for a lot of money. When the Mayor declined, they refused to leave and have fooled everyone into thinking that they work for him. It's the Gang Green members that are reaping havoc around town not the Mayor."

"It's true, I'm afraid. I'm basically a prisoner in my own offices," added Mayor MacDonald dejectedly. "I haven't been home in many years. Neither has Polly. We haven't even been outside." A look flashed between the two of them that told Alice that the Mayor and his bird had grown fond of each other during captivity.

Alice recalled the run down state of the Mayor's private house. Perhaps it had more to do with him being held prisoner than being miserly. But where were the other Council members? Again, Alice felt that the portrait paintings in the room were somehow watching her.

"So you admit to taking all of the townsfolk's money by taxing everything in sight?" She pressed on, determined to hold him to account.

"Yes, and I'm very pleased with the result." He sighed for a third time. "Let me tell you what happened. You see, many years ago, bit by bit, the Councillors of this town grew greedy and corrupt."

One of the wooden picture frames cracked loudly, sending a few splinters in the Mayor's direction. The face in the portrait was of an angry old man. *How peculiar to have one's portrait painted with such an expression of anger,* thought Alice.

"Their corrupt way of life spread to the town and soon everyone became obsessed with money. Stealing, bribery and cheating were just a means to an end as long as one didn't get caught. And of course, the councillors watched one another's backs to make sure that none of them was caught red-handed.

"I was invited to join the Council some years ago after making a name for myself in the market as a successful second-hand seller. They knew I was a shrewd businessman. I'd buy and sell anything I could get my hands on. I enjoyed it. I could see how much happier it made people to get rid of their junk for more money than they expected to get and for other people to pick up something useful for peanuts.

One man's trash is another man's treasure and all that. So I thought that if I could get into the Council, perhaps I could change things around and cure the rot from within. Sooner or later, I knew the greed and corruption would infect other parts of Wonderland."

"Needless to say, the other councillors and the Gang Green didn't take kindly to the Mayor's ideas," Polly chirped.

"At first, I had to lay low and pretend to be one of them. That's one reason why some of the townsfolk still see me as a villain. But it was the only way to get accepted onto the Council and win their trust. Once I got here, I saw things were a hundred times worse than I had feared."

One of the portraits dropped from the wall. Polly jumped into the air, sending her teacup into a pile of papers. Fortunately, the cup was empty but it still managed to scatter papers all over the floor. "Don't worry about those Polly. I have a feeling we shan't be needing them anymore."

The Mayor looked up at the angry faces in the picture frames.

"These are the portraits of all the Councillors in recent times. They wanted to have their portraits painted so that they would live on and oversee things here even after death."

"And are they all dead? They seem a bit alive to me."

"One by one, they all died. Most died of old age or over-eating. As the years go by, their faces seem to get progressively angrier. Occasionally, like today, they manage to make mischief. But nothing like the catastrophe they caused Banbury when they were alive. Take that old man there – George Porgiss."

Alice looked up at the bloated red face and body of a man in his sixties. He was literally bursting out of his tweed waistcoat and trousers and carried a half-cocked shotgun under his arm. He leered out of the picture at Alice.

"Georgie Porgie they used to call him. He got that fat eating pheasant pie and plum pudding, often at the same time. As well as swindling farmers out of their land and livestock, he would chase after all the women, whether they were married or not."

"How disgusting."

"Yes. He upset a good many women and almost as many husbands. Most were too afraid of him or the Gang Green to stand up to him. Then there's Richard York."

Jackson pointed to the painting of a man whose long, thin bearded face made him a dark and sinister individual.

"He was obsessed with making money by putting the town's children to work. He had half the town's girls and boys sent down the mines and into the rock."

"What did they mine?"

"Rocks. Richard made them polish the stones or sculpt them into farmyard animals and sell them as souvenirs to visitors passing through Banbury. The children had little time to be children and rarely saw the sun. They could only play at night by the light of the moon, which meant they didn't have much time for supper or sleep before they had to get up again and go back down the mines."

"What a horrible man."

"They also called him 'The Duke' on account of his crazy plan to build an army. Those children that were not fit enough to work in the mines were drafted into a makeshift army."

"Why didn't he use men for the army?"

"The Council needed all the skilled labour to earn money for them. Every craftsman, from carters and turners to furrowers and barrowers, earned money for the Council. Nothing got in the way of their money-making. Besides, Banbury didn't really need an army. The last trouble here was the famous guinea pig revolt of 1769. And they were crushed the same afternoon, poor mites. Anyway, Richard York had the children do drill practice. He marched them up and down hills, but being unfit, half of them perished during the march, half got injured in battle practice and half hid under their beds."

"That's three halves. You can't have three halves of something."

"Yes, you can. Three halves make one and a half."

"Yes but one and a half can't be the whole amount."

"It can be," said Polly, coming to the Mayor's rescue. "Richard York had one and a half thousand children in his army. And it was also the whole army."

"Yes but if one thousand five hundred was the total, then a half of that would be seven hundred and fifty. Five hundred would be a third."

"I see where you're going wrong," said Mayor MacDonald. "You're not factoring in the movement of children between the three groups and the subsequent overlap in segments."

"Oh, you mean like a Ven Diagram?"

"Exactly," said the Mayor, who had not heard of such a thing before. "Richard used those all the time. He never did anything by halves."

There was a rumble in the rafters and Richard York's teeth were now visible in his portrait painting. Alice was very glad he had been framed and couldn't get out.

"Have you see any children around town?" asked Mayor Jackson, hopefully.

"No! I knew there was something strange apart from the painted-on house features. And lack of money. And talking animals and telephones. No children!"

"Thanks to the Gang Green, we still don't know exactly where they are. I've heard that there aren't many in town any more, just the bad apples. I have a feeling we shan't be seeing them back here any time soon. The Gang Green are using every means to preserve their power over the town. And that means carrying on the Council's crimes to terrorise the townsfolk. History repeats itself."

That's so true, thought Alice. *Sounds just like my boring history of economics class.*

"The Council sounds like a despicable group of men," she said, wanting to change the subject back to the Mayor's taxation.

"They were. It's important you understand just how bad, Alice. Take Jack Horner up there."

One particularly frightening portrait showed a smallish, baby-faced man, whose pointed ears and long thin fingers made him look almost demonic.

"He had a stranglehold on the food and beverage industry, ironic seeing how scrawny he was."

A high-pitched wail floated around the room and the table shook, sending more papers tumbling to the floor.

"Jack Horner had a hand in all the food and drink, so between the two of them he and George Porgiss controlled the whole supply chain from cradle to grave. Jack Horner also looked after public spending and social welfare. That included social events. He was apparently the judge who awarded my mother's plum pie third place just because she wouldn't sell our farm to George Porgiss. Turns out, Jack had his finger in many pies, so to speak. Through secret deals and insider trading, he became the owner to the deeds for half the buildings in Banbury. It made me sick to my back teeth to see Jack huddled over his favourite Christmas dish - plum pie - pulling out plums with his ghoulishly long fingers. More tea, Alice?"

"No, thank you. But about those taxes..."

"Then there were the others," said the Mayor to Polly, ignoring Alice completely. "Kingston Cole. He drank, smoked and danced himself to death in some very dubious company indeed. Then Peter Stout, the father of that young hooligan, Thomas Stout."

The Mayor pointed to a painting of Peter Stout, who was dressed in pink shirt, blue jacket, green waistcoat and red trousers. He was sitting on a pumpkin the size of a horse and playing a flute. There was a crazed look in his eye as if he was about to leap out of the picture frame and seize Alice.

158

"Very talented flute player but totally useless as a town official. He used to dress that colourfully every day and eat pumpkins and pickled peppers like there was no tomorrow. Terrible problems with wind. Kept the whole house awake. When his wife tried to get him to cut down, he imprisoned her in an empty pumpkin shell to teach her a lesson. Well, she broke out rather easily of course and we never saw her again. He remarried but never really got over his first wife. That was until he studied psychiatry and psychology and learned that he was blaming others for his own problems. Went off to Hamelin in Germany to study psychotherapy and become a master flautist. Rumour was that he got beaten to death by rats. And then over there..."

"Yes, I see, the Council was dishonest!" interrupted Alice. "Things were terrible. But things are still not right in Wonderland."

"My point is, Alice, the men in these paintings have succeeded in ruining Banbury over the years. With their propaganda, they distorted all the good things past Councils did for this town and rewrote history. The people knew no better."

"You mean 'Happy is the country with no history'?" Alice was about to study History in London, so the idea of robbing people of their past was very unsettling.

"Precisely. They were able to start from a clean sheet. With the help of the Gang Green, they have made Banbury the most corrupt town in Wonderland and all living creatures have suffered beyond measure. It's only a matter of time before it spreads across Wonderland. For all I know, it may infect your world too."

"Well, how on earth does it help to take away their money?" Alice knew she was adding insult to injury but she wanted to understand what was happening now, not in the past.

"I thought that if I were patient, once I had sole control over the Council, I would be able to reverse things. But now I'm not so sure. The corruption is so deep-rooted in people's lives there is no simple or quick solution."

"Couldn't you speak to the people? Appeal to them?" asked Alice.

"I've tried. But whenever I try to make myself heard, the Gang Green step in and put a stop to it. Polly installed a telephone and connected it to loudspeakers around the market so I could speak direct to the people. But it was only recently we discovered that the Gang Green had disconnected it ages ago. They cancel all my public events. I was supposed to talk to the people this morning in the church but the Gang Green 'locked me in my bedroom', hid my clothes and then 'couldn't get the front door open'."

"The townsfolk think you overslept."

"Yes, I'm sure that's what the Gang Green told them."

"But what I still don't understand," continued Alice, "is why you insist on taking away people's money. If it's true, you can't blame them for hating you."

Mayor Jackson MacDonald stretched his arms out and gave a huge sigh, possibly the fourth or fifth whilst Alice had been in the room. She had lost count.

"That was supposed to be the key to my master plan. I got the idea at the marketplace when I was trading things with almost no money changing hands. I figured that if, as they say, money is the root of all evil, maybe we should do away with it all together. I thought that people would be happier with an economy based entirely on exchanging goods. That would take them back to the true value of things. Make them talk to each other, trust each other. I wanted them to value themselves and others as people, and things as things, not just according to a price tag. The best things in life are free. All that honesty had been forgotten in the scramble for more and more money."

"And you thought that taxing people to death would be a good idea?"

"It was the only way I could think of to remove all the money from circulation. To force people to live without it. I told the Gang Green we were collecting money from people to pay for repairs to the Council House. Some of them call me St Matthew, after the patron saint of tax collectors. They went along with it, planning to steal all the money for themselves after it had all been collected. Each night, however, I burnt most of the notes and buried most of the coins that they had collected that day. The Gang Green were mystified and frustrated at how slowly the money pile was growing, but I left just enough for them to want to go out and find more.

"I know it was a radical and painful measure but I could see no other way. Sometimes, one has to be cruel to be kind. This was the ultimate test of that. I knew the people of Banbury would suffer at first and hate me even. But if it meant that they would learn to love each other again, then it would be a small sacrifice."

Polly brushed a tear away with her wing. Alice was trying to get her head round everything she had just heard. Was it possible that she, along with the rest of Banbury, had misunderstood the Mayor so badly?

"I'm not sure I understand how it all works," said Alice, who loathed how her father would drone on about the state of the country's economy. "But that might be either the most ridiculous idea or the most brilliant one I've ever heard. It's a pity that the people of Banbury never got to hear the real story. I'm sure they'd realise how vile those Councillors were, how nasty the Gang Green is and how all along you've been trying to stamp out the evil they created."

Polly said something but it was drowned out by a collective roar as the portraits of old councillors stretched their mouths open wide to shout a stream of abuse at Alice. She couldn't make out their exact words in all the din but it was clearly a mixture of profanities and threats. The canvasses shook at the noise and small pieces of plaster fell from the ceiling.

"I have no doubt that somehow they are still poisoning Wonderland," shouted Alice above the noise. She marched over to the portrait of Peter Stout and seized the picture frame in both hands. As the face in the picture wailed and bellowed, Alice flipped the frame over. Strangely enough, the back of Peter Stout's head was superimposed on the back of the painting. His cries were muffled but it only enraged the other Councillors more. Their cries thundered and ricocheted around the walls, which gradually began to crumble.

"We can't stay here," screeched Polly, gathering up the cups and saucers onto the tray. "The whole building is collapsing.

"Leave the dishes, Polly!" said the Mayor. "I have a feeling we shan't be having afternoon tea for a while."

Polly said something back but she couldn't make her voice heard. Every time one of the paintings roared, more plaster fell from the walls or ceiling. At one particularly loud yell from Georgie Porgiss, one of the mirrors cracked and pieces of glass, sharp enough to slice through meat, rained down.

As soon as Mayor Jackson MacDonald had gathered together some essentials, like his pipe, slippers and his collection of fruit infusion bags (this took a while as he needed Polly's help to remember where he had put them), the three of them ran for the door. It was not much quieter outside the Mayor's room as bit by bit the Council House was breaking up. The Gang Green was nowhere to be seen. On the staircase, just as a large chandelier came crashing down like a crystal palace, the Mayor suddenly stopped and shouted:

"We can't use the main door. It leads onto the market square. The people are already angry at me and they'll blame me for this too. They'll lynch me."

"No they won't," screeched Polly. "That's what I've been trying to tell you for the past fifteen minutes. Just before I brought up the tea, I connected our internal speaking tube to loud speakers outside. The people of Banbury have heard everything you've told Alice."

The Mayor looked like he was about to kiss Polly and it was something Alice wasn't sure she wanted to see.

"Polly, you are so clever," said Alice.

"It's something I've been planning to do for a while now. I've been waiting in the wings for the right opportunity. And when Alice showed up, I knew it was now or never."

"Polly, I would be so lost without you," said Mayor Jackson MacDonald.

Alice was now certain the Mayor was about to kiss Polly.

"Outside everyone!" shouted Alice as a huge lump of stucco landed a foot from her foot.

"Seeing is believing," said Cheshire.

"You don't always have to see things to know they are there," chimed in Alice. "How about your body, tail and legs? I can't see them now but I know they exist."

"But that's just it, Alice. At this precise moment, they don't exist. Only my head does."

CHAPTER 8

HOME SWEAT HOME

A huge crowd had gathered outside the Council House to watch it collapse. Mayor Jackson MacDonald, Polly the secretary bird and Alice exited by the main doors with little ceremony. In fact, few noticed them and those that did only recognised Alice. The Mayor had been hidden away so long that the people had forgotten what he looked like. They had, however, listened to his story over the loudspeakers and there were cries of "Save the Mayor!" as stones fell around them. One pessimistic voice shouted, "Let's build a statue to commemorate him!" while several of the more materialistic townsfolk were volunteering to help search for the hidden coins.

Some people came up to Alice to shake her hand and thank her. She had no idea what she had done to deserve their thanks. She began to re-introduce the Mayor to people but he quickly stopped her.

"I now know it's not me that's important, Alice. It's what I've done. At least, what I've started and what the people now have to carry on doing. That's what matters.

I don't want to be recognised. I never did." Jackson MacDonald removed his chain of office and gave it to a bewildered bystander. "Here. I have a feeling I shan't be needing this anymore. From this moment on, I renounce my Mayorship. Or is it Mayordom?"

"But you have so much to talk to them about," said Alice. "They need to meet the real you."

"No-one can ever know the real me. Just like no-one will ever completely understand you, Alice."

"That's quite a scary thing to say."

"It is scary, isn't it? Tell me, would you say your parents understand you?"

"Not at all."

"Your sisters?"

"No."

"No-one is closer than family and if they don't know you, well, I rest my case. We are known and will be remembered purely by the things we do."

"But I haven't done anything."

"Not yet, Alice. But you will."

"What will I do?"

"Ah, no-one but you knows the answer to that question. You will decide how well we know you by what you do every day, all through your life. You need to seize life by the collar. Be brave and jump in with both feet. Be the best you can be."

"That's sounds like a lot of pressure. Speaking of which, don't the people of Banbury still need you around to lead them out of this mess?"

"I'm not sure I'm up to it. Let's see what the future brings. For now, I'm back to being simply Jackson MacDonald and I probably need to go and attend to my mother. Thanks to Polly, the townsfolk now know the truth. So it's up to them to make my vision come true."

Alice felt bad at having thought ill of Jackson MacDonald for so long.

"I have a confession, Mr McDonald."

"Call me Jackson, please. I suppose you're going to say you thought I was the Jabberwocky."

"Yes. How did you know?"

"Well, you're very young and it's just the kind of thing someone with a vivid imagination might think."

"Just as I was beginning to like you!" joked Alice.

The crowds around Alice had become a little blurred and she rubbed her eyes to clear her vision. But it didn't help.

"Come on, Alice," said Jackson, "there's someone I want you to meet."

Polly left Jackson's side, but not before she gave him a peck on his cheek and he ruffled her tail feathers. They would meet up again later.

Once Polly had been absorbed into the crowd, ex-Mayor Jackson MacDonald led Alice down one of the side streets leading off the square. He was so happy, he almost bounced along. Before long, everything around them was quiet and calm.

"You know, Alice, I do believe the people of Banbury will be fine without money, especially now they know why it was done."

"I do hope you're right," said Alice.

She hadn't been down this road before, not that it looked much different from the other streets. She had become quite attached to the house facades with everything painted on as opposed to being real.

"Will you repaint your house?" she asked.

"Yes. I'm so looking forward to leading a normal life with Polly."

Alice thought that Jackson was stretching the meaning of the word "normal" but she was very happy for him.

"So who was it you wanted me to meet?"

"You'll see. It's a bit of a walk but there's not much that a good stiff walk won't cure."

"That's funny, that's just what my father says."

After some minutes, the rows of painted houses ended abruptly in fields. To the right, the countryside was a patchwork of various crops – rape seed, wheat, barley, potatoes, was that a rice field? Delicious squares of browns and yellows and greens mingled in steep contrast to the endless stretch of rich green grass and deciduous forest to the left. Above, white clouds billowed across a deep blue sky like sails on the ocean.

"This is my idea of heaven," said Alice.

"I thought it might be," replied Jackson. "But of course, heaven is different for every person. For someone with hay fever this would be hell."

"Don't spoil it for me," said Alice in mock anger, for she knew Jackson was just teasing her.

"Can we walk a bit more slowly?" asked Jackson. "I'm still wearing slippers."

"Yes, I noticed." That was another annoying thing her father did.

After a mile or so, they turned left into a sandy lane that led through the grassy fields towards the woods. Soon, great oaks and old elm trees provided a thick canopy overhead, yet enough sunlight filtered through to make the glade a glorious garden of gold. A short way in, the lane widened and then ended in a pair of rusty wrought iron gates that spanned a gap between red brick walls either side. A large sign above the door read: SWEATLANDS - MORE CARE FOR MORE PEOPLE.

"Is that pronounced 'sweat' as in 'wet'?"

"It's supposed be 'sweet' as in 'cheat'. Sweetlands. What an unfortunate spelling error."

"Someone lives way out here?" asked Alice.

"More than one person. You'll see."

Above a doorbell was a small plaque, which read: "ONLY FOR PRESSING MATTERS"

"Well that makes sense," said Alice.

"Probably the only thing that does in this place," quipped Jackson. He pressed the button and the gates swung open, creaking as if they had been deliberately left unoiled.

"It's an old gate," said Jackson.

"Then they should have called this place Aldgate."

They walked along a driveway bordered by large yew and box bushes. The yellow gravel crunched underfoot.

Around a corner, the gravel driveway culminated in a large red brick mansion with a white door and white window frames.

"I had this place built with some of the money that I didn't burn. It was a venture to house those people of Banbury that were too old or fragile to look after themselves. I had seen how we were treating our old folk at the end of their road and it wasn't nice."

Alice wondered if Jackson included his own mother in this group of people. *If Banbury treats its old folk anything like it treats its animals and children, then they must be in trouble*, she thought.

"This rest home was intended as a kind of a stop gap, until Banbury was able to resurrect itself and the people look after one another properly. But that might take a little longer than I had hoped."

"It's a wonderful idea. Perhaps the town could copy it for other unfortunate groups, like old or sick animals. Or orphans."

"Maybe. Your heart is in the right place, Alice."

"I'm not so sure. Someone in Wonderland told me I wear it on my sleeve."

"Maybe that's the right place."

"Possibly. But I tend to say things in the wrong way at the wrong time."

"Well at least you say something. Many people go through life without saying anything."

"Perhaps they're just shy, like my sisters."

"Perhaps. But in my experience, it's very often because they are afraid what others may think of them. Never be afraid of saying what you really feel, Alice. And remember, the older one gets, the stronger the fear of looking stupid becomes."

"Can older people start to look so silly they appear to be animals?" asked Alice.

"What an odd thing to say."

"It's much quieter than normal," noted Jackson with a frown. "Last time I visited, a lot of the residents and staff were outside on the lawn. Now the doors and windows are all shut even though it's a beautiful day. Let's see if anyone's in. They may have all gone to the seaside."

Jackson pulled a large brass handle that dangled on the end of a rope. From inside the house, they heard a voice shout "Ow! There's someone at the door. Hurry up, before they ring again!"

The door opened and a very tall, thin and rather ugly middle-aged nurse looked down her nose at them. "Mayor MacDonald. What are you doing here? We weren't expecting you."

"Evidently not. But, I would nevertheless like to come in and show Alice around, if that's all right with you?"

"Sorry. Now is not a very good time. We are overseeing an extensive renovation to the building."

"A renovation? As founder of this home, I should have been informed about any renovation. What are you doing?"

She hesitated. "Changing all the locks."

A bad excuse is better than none, thought Alice, but decided to let Jackson handle the nurse.

"Well, that's not a problem," said Jackson. "I'm sure we can see the part of the facility that's unlocked."

"Changing all the locks as well as changing the beds," added the nurse.

"Changing the beds is hardly a renovation. Most people do it at least once a week."

"By changing, I mean we're throwing all the old beds out and buying new ones."

"Whatever for? They can't be old yet."

The nurse looked back and forth between the Mayor and Alice, clearly considering how much to tell them.

"According to our research, old people..."

"The elderly," said Jackson, correcting her.

"Quite. The elderly are shrinking. On average, each old ... aged person is using only eighty per cent of the length of his or her bed. And sixty-eight per cent of the width. By giving them smaller beds, we can fit ... we can care for more people."

"You mean to say you are squeezing more people into one room?" asked Jackson.

"Of course not," said the nurse. "That would be barbaric. We have a policy of one person per cell ... I mean room."

"But surely," said Alice. "If you have the same number of rooms, then you don't save any space at all."

"Did I forget to say we are lowering the ceilings and moving the walls in too?"

"I want to see what's happening," said Jackson, pushing past the nurse and looking angrier than Alice had seen him all day. Once they were inside, Alice took stock of her surroundings. It reminded her of the entrance hall to her old school. There was a lot of dark wood panelling and corridors leading off to the right and to the left. Like the branches of an old tree, the corridors sprouted rooms and smaller corridors on both sides along their length. Directly in front of them was an old wooden staircase leading to the next floor, where Alice knew there would be a similar labyrinth of corridors and rooms.

It was then that Alice noticed an old man in a dressing gown standing behind the open front door. A long and taut piece of string tied to the big toe on his right foot led to a hole in the wall and presumably was connected to the outside doorbell handle. He gave Alice a please-don't-ring-the-bell-again look.

"I don't see any sign of the renovation," said Jackson.

"We haven't started yet. The builders are coming in an hour's time. Or it's their day off, I'm not sure which. But it's a highly inconvenient time."

"Inconvenient for whom?" asked Jackson, suspecting that the nurse had her own agenda for preventing them from seeing more. "I'm sorry but I insist that I see some of the residents. As Chairman of the Board of this elderly people's home I believe I am within my rights to demand this."

"Very well. On your head be it. Follow me." She stopped and smiled sarcastically. "Welcome to Sweatlands."

"Sweetlands," corrected Jackson.

The nurse gave Jackson a tired look and set off at such a pace that it was hard for Alice to keep up. They passed half a dozen doors on either side before the nurse stopped abruptly and produced a key.

"This is Mr Percy."

Alice thought it was a strange name for a key until she realised the nurse was talking about the man inside the locked room.

"We have to keep him behind lock and key for his own safety and the safety of others," she added, in response to the look on Jackson MacDonald's face.

The door opened inwards to reveal a small room with a simple bed, writing desk and chair. In one corner was a rusty enamel chamber pot and in the other a dirty mop. Sitting on the bed was a thin, haggard man of least eighty, holding is head in his hands. He had no legs and in their place, someone had tied two table legs to his stumps. Alice couldn't help wondering if they were Chippendale. On his head was a small red hat that resembled a cockerel's comb.

"Mr Percy, you have visitors. Now sit up and behave."

"Cock-a-doodle-doo!" crowed Mr Percy, raising his face to the ceiling. Mr Percy was smiling. "My cock's crowing this morning, all right."

"We don't want to know about that, thank you very much!" chided the nurse.

"Hello, My Percy," said Alice.

Mr Percy leered at Alice and made an eerie cooing noise.

"Would you care for a dance, Alice?" he cooed.

"No she wouldn't!" shouted the nurse, stepping between them.

"I used to dance you know," continued the old man with a wink. "I used to dance with my wife. A right old time of it we had. Until she lost her favourite dancing shoes," he said sadly. "She got so depressed she wouldn't dance with me anymore. Had to dance on my own. Then just when she got interested again, I lost my fiddling sticks. Not much use to her without those, am I? By the time I'd found them again, she'd done a runner. So now I dance with others, don't I? So how about it, Alice?"

He grinned a toothless grin and jumped up on his table legs. He was surprisingly fleet of foot for an old man on table legs. Before Alice had time to react, the nurse had pushed Mr Percy back on to the bed with the dirty mop and was ushering the rest of them out of the room. She locked the door behind them and glared at the visitors.

"I told you! Mad as a hatter," she exclaimed. "If I hadn't intervened, who knows what mischief he would have wrought."

"I felt a bit sorry for him," said Alice.

Jackson was visibly shaken. "I can't see how we're helping a lonely old man by locking him up in solitary confinement. If anything, it could make him worse."

"Are you a doctor?" asked the nurse and without waiting added. "I thought not."

They stopped a few rooms farther down.

"Meet Jonathan Thomas," said the nurse, flinging the door open. "He's in perfectly good shape, if you ignore the fact that he's as bonkers as Mr Percy."

The room was smaller and newer. The ceiling was so low that Alice couldn't have entered without stooping. Even the walls seemed closer together.

"You call this renovating?" said Jackson. "Even the bed's smaller. And where did the window go?

"More care for more people. That was the motto you came up with yourself, Mayor. I don't know who could argue with that."

"Well, certainly not the bank, if you are charging money from more and more people," said Jackson, a little too sarcastically for Alice's taste. "Come to think of it, are the people of Banbury still using money to pay for their board here?"

"No."

"Well, I'm glad to hear that."

"They don't have money any more, so we've had to take on people from other towns, who do have money."

"What have you done to those poor people that can no longer afford to stay here?" asked Alice.

"Nothing."

"So you're looking after them free of charge?"

"No. I mean we're doing nothing for them. Their relatives came to collect them. In the case of Mr Thomas, who doesn't have anyone, I'm sure he'll find his own way out sooner or later, when he gets hungry enough."

Jackson slumped against the wall. He was clearly shouldering some of the blame. "It wasn't supposed to be like this."

"It's so wrong," said Alice bluntly to the nurse. "You're turning your back on poor people. And it's them who need help the most."

"Rubbish!" said the nurse. "The wealthy have more problems than the poor. They need to be cared for plus they have the added burden of finding ways to spend their money, which their relatives are invariably trying to get at. Sweatlands is ideally suited to help them with their troubles. People with few possessions only have to worry about themselves. It's so much easier for them. It's the rich who need our care."

Alice couldn't believe her ears. Perhaps that's why her tongue seemed unable to respond.

Until this moment, Jonathan Thomas had lain prostrate on his under-sized bed. But now he sat up and let the light from the corridor illuminate his features. He was, like all the other residents, very old. He had a distant look in his eye, as though he was not aware of what was happening around him and couldn't make the effort to find out. He wore a white nightgown, which had begun to fray and turn grey through constant use. From under the nightgown protruded one human leg and one chair leg. Alice thought this one could be Rococo.

"Hello, Mr Thomas," said Alice.

"It was the goose, you know," said Jonathan Thomas, his pale blue eyes momentarily lucid. "He visited us during the night. Not me, my wife. He tricked her, cajoled her, brought all kinds of gifts and promised her more. How could I compete with that?"

The nurse made large circles with her forefinger against her temple.

"And he was young too. Much younger than me. And stronger. He asked me if I prayed to God every night and when I said most nights but not every night, he dragged me down the stairs by my left leg. I lost it."

Jonathan Thomas tapped his table leg.

"That's when I bumped my head and started to lose other things."

"Marbles?" suggested the nurse.

"Yes, I lost my marbles, my train set, my toy soldiers. I haven't seen them in years. And my wife, Lydia. Lost her too. Goodness knows..."

"As you see," said the nurse, shutting the door on a bewildered Jonathan Thomas mid-sentence, "we do what we can for them. But it's mostly making them comfortable during their final months. Or in some cases, years," she added and rolled her eyes. "You need a lot of patience in this job."

"I'd say you already have too many," said Alice, barking up the wrong end of the stick.

"It's quite preposterous how you treat them," said Jackson. "Last time I visited, everyone was happy. People were reading, talking, going for walks in the grounds."

"And when did you visit last? Five years ago? Times have changed since then, Mayor."

"And not for the better. By the way, what is your name?"

The nurse stopped in her tracks and looked Jackson in the eyes. She waited before answering. "Foster. Nurse Fiona Foster."

"I knew it. You're Doctor Foster's sister. My sister Gillian was engaged to your brother."

"And he's now dead as a doornail thanks to your sister."

"How come?"

"My brother was so besotted with her that he travelled all the way to Gloucester to buy her a ring. If he hadn't gone there, he would never have fallen into that puddle."

"That was hardly her fault."

"Nevertheless."

"So is that why you are running my home like a prison camp? Avenging your brother's death by sabotaging the lives of our elderly people? I demand to see Mr Shafto and get to the bottom of this."

Nurse Foster flashed Jackson a cruel smile. "Mr Shafto? Mr Robert Shafto? Are you sure?"

"Absolutely. Take me to him."

"Very well."

As the nurse led them farther down the never-ending corridor, Jackson MacDonald talked quietly to Alice.

"Robert Shafto is the Chief Executive Officer here. You'll like him. He used to run Halfway House many years ago. Grew this amazing garden of fruits and flowers and other plants made of gold, silver and jewels."

"Yes, I visited Halfway House," whispered Alice. "I heard he fell in love with a Spanish princess and sailed overseas to find her."

"He did. Tragic it was. He went dressed in his finest clothes and laden with gifts for his princess. But by the time he found her she was already married to her Spanish gardener. Ironic tragedy. Or is it tragic irony? When Robert returned, he couldn't face Halfway House, so I asked him to run Sweetlands."

Alice was beginning to think that "Sweatlands" might be a more appropriate name.

"E voila! The big man himself!" said Nurse Foster. She opened the door of another tiny new room. An elderly bearded man was hunched at a writing desk, the ceiling barely an inch above his head. He hummed a melody Alice knew but couldn't place.

"When should I harvest the nuts?" said the old man, without taking his gaze from the ledger he was writing in.

"Bobby?" said Jackson. "Bobby Shafto? It's me Jackson. Bobby? What's happened to you?"

"It's all wrong!" continued the old man. "Nobody gathers nuts in May, it's totally the wrong time of year. It doesn't make sense! There must be a deeper meaning to it all."

"Bobby, it's me, Jackson."

Robert Shafto looked up but saw no-one, just a world of blank pages in his ledger waiting to be filled.

"It's too cold for nuts in May. In fact, England is always too cold for nuts. Unless...unless...they are mistakenly referring to the underground tuber of the pignut - *Conopodium majus.* You know of it perhaps?"

Robert Shafto was not directing his question at anyone in particular but Alice felt obliged to answer. Especially as she was sure she heard the words "Underground" and "Tube".

"I know all the names of the London Underground stations, but I haven't heard of anything like 'Connor Podium'. Could it be that they haven't built it yet?"

"My dear girl, I speak of a small perennial herb," Robert explained further. "Some people call it a groundnut as you can eat it as a root vegetable, even cultivate it as it grows quite sparsely in the wild. Its tubers naturally grow underground and it's just possible they mistook them for chestnuts. Though only an expert gardener could tell the difference."

Alice was disappointed that she wouldn't get to discuss the London Underground with someone but she was fascinated at how dedicated the man seemed to be to solving the problem of a simple nursery rhyme.

"Perhaps," said Alice, trying to be helpful, "the real message is about mulberries." She knew the words to the tune he was humming to be not about nuts in May but about dancing round a mulberry bush. Perhaps he was barking up the wrong tree. She recited the "Here we go round the mulberry bush" poem for him.

"*...on a cold and frosty morning.*"

Robert Shafto had clearly heard Alice's voice because he looked around the room trying to locate the source. He answered without looking at her.

"Interesting. You're a clever little thing. But not as clever as you think because this creates a whole new mystery. You see, mulberries don't grow on bushes. They grow on trees. And they certainly don't grow in freezing weather. It's another riddle. But I'm getting closer. And you've been of great help. Thank you," he added, looking up at the ceiling and then scribbling furiously to document this new piece of the puzzle.

Nurse Foster sighed and rolled her eyes again. "Mr Shafto hears voices."

"Of course, he does," answered Alice, angrily. "He heard mine. We all hear voices when someone speaks to us!" She was getting quite cross with the nurse, who seemed set on ridiculing the residents.

"I can't help thinking it has something to do with Japan," interrupted Robert Shafto. "Because in Japan people wear kimonos. And kimonos are made of silk. And silk is made by silk worms, which live on mulberry leaves. So if we don't have mulberry trees, the people of Japan might be furious with us."

There was an odd logic to Robert Shafto's train of thought. But it was a kind too strange for Alice to think that he would ever do little more than write nonsense in his ledger. It was a shame because Alice was beginning to like Mr Shafto.

"Or had they simply begun to use the word *nuts* after corrupting the original phrase about 'gathering *knots* in May' - the tradition of gathering bunches of flowers to celebrate the end of winter?"

They left Mr Shafto to his life's work. Once they were back out in the corridor, Jackson was clearly in a state of shock.

"How did Mr Shafto get like that? What did you do to him? What happened to make him lose his mind?"

"I've no idea," said the nurse. "But if you ask me, anyone that sails overseas in search of love is already doolally."

They went farther down the corridor, deeper into the warren of rooms. Room after room. There was something about the sheer number of rooms that unsettled Alice; a distant memory that she needed to remember, but which was just out of reach, hiding behind the corners of her brain just as she caught sight of it.

She was shaken out of her own thoughts by the sight of a large man carrying a bed from one room to another. He was dressed in a grey uniform, making him look more like a warden than an orderly. What made Alice's blood curdle was the fact that she recognised him as one of the Gang Green. If their members worked at Sweatlands too, there was a good chance that they were behind the corruption here. Alice was about to ask Jackson if he had seen what she had, when he spoke up.

"I can't just stand by and watch this. You are keeping these poor people prisoners."

"Rich people," corrected the nurse.

"Whatever. Elderly people need social contact just like the rest of us."

"And they have it. You haven't seen the kitchen and canteen area yet. That's where they interact with each other."

"And then you send them back to their rooms?"

"If there's one free, yes."

"What do you mean?"

"Well, we've taken in so many paying inmates ... residents sorry, that there aren't quite enough rooms for everyone. So at any one point in time we round up and herd a number of them into the canteen. It costs something to feed them of course but that's covered ten times over by the additional fees we secure."

Jackson held his head in his hands and moaned. "Show me."

A few turns left and right led them to a large white room, bare but for metal tables and chairs. Most of them were occupied by elderly men and women in their pyjamas and dressing gowns. Amidst the din of chairs being scraped noisily across floor, the residents were playing cards, talking or eating. Nurse Foster took Jackson and

Alice to a long serving counter at the far end of the room and introduced them to an old lady, who was dishing out ladles of weak soup onto flat plates. Half of it seemed to end up on the trays or on the counter.

"Nell is one of the few residents we still have from Banbury," said the nurse. "We let her stay here because she works for free. Tell them, Nell."

Nell was dressed in a large white apron and tall white hat. She gave a toothless smile and spoke in a crackly voice as she continued to slop the soup out.

"I'm a Banbury baker by trade. That's how I got the job of cook here at Sweat House."

"Sweatlands," corrected Nurse Foster.

"Sweetlands," said Jackson, half-heartedly.

Alice could well imagine Nell hawking her wares on Baker Street.

"I left the bakery to work at the Unfair as the original Baker girl. I was dressed up as the Baker, I was. Mandy was the Butcher and Sally the Candlestick-maker. Together we was the Splash Girls. I earned the same in one evening as what I earned in a whole month in the bakery. Then I got old and the owners said the men didn't want to pay to see me, let alone … well, you know. Now I'm cooped up in this madhouse, but at least I got a roof over my head and three square meals a day, don't I?"

"The meal looks round to me," said the nurse, fed up with Nell's whining.

"And that's just one reason why I wouldn't touch the stuff," replied Nell. "They call it pease pudding. Lumps of fat and hard peas in water, if you ask me. Disgusting! I make sure I eats my fair share back there in the kitchen. The only reason they lets me stay here is that I'm the only one who would agree to make such cheap muck."

"Don't they get any other food?" asked Alice. "Fruit, cakes, biscuits?" Alice couldn't imagine life without any one of those.

"Oh yes. If you count the rotten apples they picks off the ground. And the cakes and biscuits that I make out of flour and water."

"Stop exaggerating, Nell!" shouted the nurse. "She's exaggerating. We send a man to Drury Lane every week to buy fresh bakery goods."

"You mean that simple Simon? Most of the time, all he comes back with is a black eye for trying to pinch something off the muffin man. Anyway, any pie or biscuit that does find its way back here gets gobbled up by the staff. They even mark their initials on them because they're afraid someone will steal their food."

"Nonsense! Look around you. Everyone has food. Most of the plates are already empty."

"Because most of it runs off the plates to begin with," snarled Nell. "Look at Mr Spratt over there. The skinny man. Not allowed to eat fat on account of his heart problem, so he only has the liquid and hard peas. Which means his wife, the gigantic lady opposite him, has to eat the fat and gristle if she's to survive. And woe betide anyone who leaves some food on their plate. They gets it served back to them the next day."

"Some like it hot, some like it cold," said the nurse.

"But not many still likes it nine days' old, do they?" said Nell. "No wonder so many of them are having 'accidents' in here."

"People are getting hurt?" asked Jackson.

"She's exaggerating again," butted in the nurse.

"Take old Mr Rogers, over there. They forced him to walk around the garden even though it was pouring with rain. Got such a cold that his nose got blocked up, didn't it. Snored so loudly it woke him up and he banged his head so hard it knocked him out. Couldn't even get up the following morning. Locked up, blocked up, knocked out. Never been the same since."

"Hardly our fault if he forgot to put his coat on!" said the nurse.

"And how about old Mr John over there? They forced him to eat the same dumpling for a fortnight. So mouldy it was he got food poisoning. Didn't know what time of day it was. Went to bed with half his clothes on then got up and came down to breakfast stark naked. And they never recovers after that, you know."

"Nor did the people that saw it!" snorted the nurse.

"I've seen enough!" shouted Jackson.

"That's exactly what I said," commented Nell.

"I'm going to stay here to set things right. I'm taking over this place and I'm not leaving until everything is right again."

"Well, you should fit in well here. I see you already have your slippers on and your pipe handy," she scoffed, and rolled her eyes yet again.

Alice was lamenting Jackson's decision to stay behind at Sweatlands. She knew it was the right thing to do but this meant that he would no longer be around to support her. She had got used to his company and had been hoping he would help her return home.

"I'm sorry, Alice. I can't leave these people to face Nurse Foster and whoever else is in on this. I'll send for help from town. I'm sure people will come to help me repair all the damage that's been done here and deal with the Gang Green. I'll send some of the people on after you to help you too."

Jackson looked around for the nurse but she had managed to slide away unnoticed. She had left a bunch of keys behind on the counter and Jackson seized them just before Nell slapped a large dollop of soup on top of them.

"I understand," said Alice. "It's time I was going anyway. I miss home and I need to get back. I don't see what I can do here and I feel I've outstayed my welcome."

"You've saved Banbury," said Jackson and kissed the top of Alice's head, "and rescued Polly and I. I don't know how to repay you."

Alice looked at the tips of her dirty shoes. She felt humbled by Jackson's gratitude yet frustrated and helpless about what to do next.

"Actually, I do," added Jackson. "I almost forgot the reason I brought you here. There's someone I want you to meet."

Without further explanation, Jackson took Alice's hand and led her away from the canteen, down one of the corridors. More rooms. More doors. Why did Alice think that they would be better painted white? They turned left, descended two flights of stairs and continued along a long dimly lit passage with no doors either side. At the end was one solitary door.

"This used to be the largest, most exclusive room in the building," said Jackson.

"But why is it so far away from everything else?"

"It's what he wanted."

Jackson wiped pease pudding off one of the keys and unlocked the door.

"Cheshire?" he whispered into the dark.

Alice breathed deeply and smiled as the wall of water rose above her. She marvelled at the mermaids, serpents and other fantastic creatures silhouetted against the blue sky behind.

CHAPTER 9

ALL ENDS IF NOT ALWAYS VERY WELL

The staff had already renovated the Cheshire Cat's room. The room had no light of its own, so the back half was in darkness. The little light that did get in from the corridor showed Alice and Jackson that the walls had been moved in and ceiling lowered. It was tiny.

"Cheshire, dear friend?"

"Mayor Jackson?" came a familiar voice from the darkness.

Out of the gloom slowly floated a face Alice had not seen for years. She had indeed talked to the Cheshire Cat on the telephone but had no idea that he was shut up in a dungeon. She recognised his broad feline face despite his fur being dirty and bedraggled. He was much older too as his grey whiskers testified. Despite his age and condition, his white teeth beamed in a familiar grin and his eyes, though bloodshot, were as big as ever. Of his body there was no sign but this did not alarm Alice. She was sure it would appear when it was ready.

"Alice!" cried the Cheshire Cat. "Am I glad to see you!"

Alice ran and gave the Cheshire Cat's large head a long hug. He smelled bad.

"Why did they shut you up like this?" cried Alice, angrily.

"Because I asked them too. As I'm sure you remember, Alice, I have a habit of losing my body now and then, also some other bits. I'm used to it. Sometimes, I lose everything but my grin. But one day, when I noticed that I was also losing my mind I couldn't bear it. It was so degrading. So I must have asked them to keep me in this room. I asked for a telephone so I could talk to people on those occasions when my mind was all there. Here, I mean."

"Poor Cheshire," said Alice, her arms around his shaggy head.

"When I learned you were in Wonderland," he continued, "I wanted to talk to you. I knew that you would try to help us and I wanted Wonderland to help you at the same time. I suspected the two might be connected and I was right."

"I wish you were right. But I'm no closer to getting home."

"Well that's what I wanted to talk to you about. You are. You see, the road doesn't go on for much longer. It ends in the sea. And as you don't want to retrace your steps to the beginning of the road, you'll have to go on to the end. So it stands to reason that the end is exactly where you'll find the start of the way back to your world."

"Why do you believe that?" said Jackson. "There are other towns and villages in Wonderland. So there must be countless roads Alice could take."

"Have you seen them? I'm not so sure there are. Seeing is believing, you know."

"You don't always have to see things to know they are there," chimed in Alice. "How about your body, tail and legs? I can't see them now but I know they exist."

"But that's just it, Alice. At this precise moment they don't exist. Only my head exists. Just like at this exact moment, only this room and corridor and the three of us exist. No other rooms, no Banbury, no other towns. Nothing else exists and you have no reason to believe it does."

"Then how am I to believe that there is a road I cannot see and it will take me home?"

"You don't have to believe. But you can hope. That's a very different prospect. Sometimes it's all we have. And hope is more powerful than belief because it leaves the door open to many more options."

"If it were not for hope, the heart would break," said Jackson.

"Exactly," said Cheshire. "I have no reason to believe I will ever see my ears again but I hope something changes so that I will."

"Like someone gives you a mirror?" suggested Alice.

"Now you've got it!"

Alice wasn't at all sure she had it. Her parents were constantly telling her to believe in herself. They never mentioned hoping in herself. On the other hand, she had no reason to believe they were right and rather hoped they weren't.

One thing that Alice did believe was that she was good at thinking on her feet. To be honest, she didn't see how it was much different from thinking while sitting down, which she could also do. She trusted her instincts and right now they were telling her to take Cheshire away from this place.

"Come with me to the end of the road, Cheshire. Leave your horrible room and let's have a last adventure together. It'll be like old times."

The Cheshire Cat's grin widened even more.

"I was hoping you would say that."

True to his word, Jackson MacDonald stayed on at Sweatlands to try and rectify all that Nurse Foster, the Gang Green and a few wayward staff members had spoilt over the years. It was a huge task. His last words to Alice were: "I have a feeling I shan't be going back to Banbury for a while."

Alice was sad to say goodbye as she had come to depend on Jackson's calmness and sensibility when all around was in turmoil. He had given her courage and confidence. She was in no doubt that he would succeed in enlisting volunteers from town to help him put things right and eventually be reunited with Polly and live happily ever after in his town house.

Outside the gates of Sweatlands, Alice and part of the Cheshire Cat found the lane that led back to the road but something in the air had changed. It was as if the heady joy of summer had transformed into the melancholy of autumn. The leaves had a brown tinge to them and while not yet falling from the trees, they seemed to be hanging on by their fingertips. There was a subtle bite in the cool breeze. The countryside was still beautiful but in a sad way.

When they reached the road, Alice observed more changes. On the right of the road, the multi-coloured patchwork of fields had become a mixture of wasteland and warehouses that ran as far as the eye could see. The endless stretch of grassland and forest on the left was now broken by groups of houses and piles of logs.

"It's all changed."

At that precise moment, only the Cheshire Cat's eyes, nose and mouth hung in the air and Alice had to wait for his ears to appear so he could hear her.

"I said 'Everything's changed'."

"I can lip read, you know. I'm not dead quite yet!" chided Cheshire, then continued good-naturedly. "I think this is probably a totally different place to the one you were in before you entered the Home."

"Oh no. It's the same place but things aren't the same."

"What I mean is that if the road indeed ceased to exist while you were in Sweatlands, I would be quite surprised if it bore the slightest resemblance at all to the one before."

Alice felt tears begin to well up in her eyes. It felt as though she was losing something she couldn't put her finger on. She was being forced to say goodbye to a part of Wonderland she would never see again.

"Come, come, Alice. Crying won't help. Look on the bright side. You're soon at the end of your journey in Wonderland. With any luck you'll be home soon."

"I so want to be home right now with my family. And I never want to leave there. Ever. Not even to go to college."

"I'm not sure that's possible. We all grow up, grow older. Things change and we have to change with them. We can't stop Time."

"I know. It's just that for years one waits for things to change. Then suddenly they do and everything changes far too quickly. It's almost as if Time is playing tricks on us."

"Well it can't be easy being Time. Imagine having to find a time and place for everything. I'm sure Time makes mistakes occasionally and has to make it fly along to catch up."

Alice and the Cheshire Cat walked together down the road away from Sweatlands and Banbury (well, Alice walked, the Cheshire Cat sort of floated from place to place). She walked slowly, partly because she was feeling tired and sad. And partly because she knew they were almost at the end of the road and there was no need to hurry. She believed, no hoped that home was close now.

"I'm so weary," said Alice.

"It's good to be wary," replied Cheshire, whose ears had not quite materialised. "Only fools rush in. You look tired too. How about we stop for a rest?"

Alice rested her head against Cheshire's fur and dozed off.

She knew she was dreaming, but try as she might, she could not stop her nightmare about the tiger from continuing.

She was standing at one end of the long banquet table, while the starving tiger, which blamed Alice for the loss of its stripes, effortlessly stepped up onto a bench and leapt up onto the far end of the table. As it slowly padded along towards Alice, other people on the table either fled from its path or were mauled by its sharp claws or teeth. It's a dream within a dream, Alice said to herself. Nothing can harm me.

Alice waited until the tiger was busy with one of the courtiers about half way down the table, before jumping down to the floor and running towards a huge fireplace, which had a high and broad mantelpiece, big enough for her to climb onto. The tiger spotted her sudden movement and went into a frenzy. People screamed even more loudly and ran in all directions. It was pandemonium. Some followed Alice towards the fireplace, forming a barrier between her and the tiger. The tiger ran in the same direction, striking people down. Alice knew she had to reach the mantelpiece before the other people. For every person the tiger had to deal with, she felt both relief and guilt.

She reached the fireplace and jumped up, her hands and elbows resting on the mantelpiece. But she was too weak to haul herself up. Placing one foot on a coal scuttle, she pushed herself up and managed to heave herself into a kneeling position. Her face was pressed against the cold surface of a large mirror. Both legs below her knees stuck out and she could feel the tiger's hot breath on her skin. She screamed as loud as she could to wake herself from the dream but it didn't work. She willed the mirror to let her pass through to a safer place but it remained solid. She lifted one leg and was just in the process of standing upright on the mantelpiece when she felt the sharp claws of the tiger sink into her ankle.

Alice woke, tossing and turning. Without arms or legs to hold her, all the Cheshire Cat could do was gently lick her face to console her. In fact, the Cheshire's Cat's mouth was all that was present. Alice had never been licked by just a mouth before and she found it disconcerting and certainly not consoling.

"Has Dinah never licked your face before?" asked Cheshire, when his nose, eyes and the rest of his face had reappeared.

"Of course, but there was a head, body and legs attached. But thank you all the same. It's the thought that counts."

It was a long while before Alice's nerves settled down and she was back to her normal self. She didn't speak of the nightmare and Cheshire didn't ask. They both knew in some bad dreams one just had to be there to appreciate how real and terrifying they were.

When at last Alice rose, there was a freshness and saltiness in the air. A lone seagull glided on the air currents, calling out to unseen friends. Not far ahead, the landscape became flat and something twinkled on the horizon. Water perhaps. The sea?

For the most part, Alice and the Cheshire Cat discussed Alice adventures. She told him about the animals on the train, the sweets that turned to coins, the Winter Forest and the mud flats. She knew something special had happened to her in the Forest but she couldn't quite remember what it was. She described Mary, Humphrey Dunfry, Mrs MacDonald and all the people she had met in Banbury and Sweatlands. She even showed him her black feather but was unable to recall where or how she had come by it.

"This is the one thing that got me through the wilderness," Alice said as her eyes welled up with tears. "And I don't know why."

"I'll tell you about it one day," said the Cheshire Cat. "I'm fairly certain that it's connected to an important event in your life."

Alice also told him about what had been happening to her back home; her studies, her father's illness and how conflicted she was about leaving for London. It felt good to talk to someone else about everything. Even when only the Cheshire Cat's mouth was visible and she knew she was just talking to herself. If not halved, her troubles were shared and she felt better for it. She also asked Cheshire about his time in the dark cell and was glad to notice that the more he talked, the more he became his old self. *Very old self*, she mused. Without realising, Alice had cheered up and found she was looking towards the future with renewed hope.

Gradually, the distant sparkles grew in number and size until Alice could make out a vast sea of dark blue ahead. Large waves made a steady booming sound as they crashed rhythmically onto the beach. A wide stretch of yellow sand separated the sea from the rest of Wonderland and there was a tangy smell of salt and seaweed in the air.

"I wonder which of the seven seas this is," Alice said aloud. "It's beautiful."

"The future is rarely as bad as it seemed beforehand," said Cheshire. "In most cases."

The road ended in a sudden and most unspectacular way. A few rows of cobblestones across the road was the only indication that Alice had come to the end of her journey. The sandy beach stretched both ways along the shore. Monster waves of turquoise and green crashed onto the sloping shoreline a stone's throw away. The seashore was gloriously desolate but that also meant there was no sign as to what Alice should do or where she should go next.

"Where to now?" she said, hopeful that Cheshire would have an answer.

"I'm not sure," said Cheshire. "Sorry I'm not much help this time. You see, I'm at the end of the road myself, in more ways than one." There was a sadness in his voice. "I can't go any further. I'm afraid you'll have to take the last steps yourself. But don't worry, you've done well on your own so far."

There was panic in Alice's voice. "I'm not sure I can survive on my own."

Cheshire smiled. "You know you can, Alice."

His words frightened her. Where was he going? Why was she once again faced with being alone? She placed her arms around his head, only to feel a part of it vanishing beneath her fingers.

"Take care of yourself, Alice. You won't see me again."

There was a dreadful finality to his words. Alice didn't want to believe Cheshire was dying so she hoped he wasn't. She buried her face in the thick fur of his cheek. She didn't want him to go. There were still so many things to discuss with him. She should have used their time on the road more wisely, to talk about more important things. Like feelings. *Cabbages and Kings*. It was all too late now.

She screwed up her eyes tightly to stop the tears from wetting his fur. She listened to the sound of her own breathing and wondered. *If Cheshire's body indeed ceases to exist when it isn't visible, how does he continue to breathe?* But this was Wonderland after all, where things didn't have to make sense.

A new sound joined her breathing and the crashing of waves. It was an unnatural, unpleasant noise that had no business interrupting their farewell. It was the faint but growing noise of a large group of people. Alice looked up and saw a line of figures marching side by side along the road from the direction of Banbury. The dust cloud suggested many more people followed them.

She could feel Cheshire tense up under her touch. "It's time, Alice. Time to think only of yourself. You have to go now," he whispered.

"Go where?"

Angry shouts rose up and it looked as though some of the throng bore staves and pitchforks. Alice could think of no reason why they should be angry at her.

Cheshire's voice was now louder, more insistent. "You have to go, Alice. You're in danger."

Alice looked into his large watery eyes and for the first time saw fear in the magical creature. Yet his enormous grin hinted at the possibility of a way out before the mob was upon her. But which way? Left or right along the beach?

As Cheshire's face began to fade his fur became coarse to the touch. Alice was left holding loose hairs in her hand, which in turn melted away. She could feel the creature's hard, leathery skin underneath. Soon, just his big sad eyes and grinning mouth hung in the air. Alice took her hands away before she found out what they felt like to the touch. This time, there was something different, heart-breaking, about the way he faded away and she feared that she really would not see him again. He had only just left his dungeon, yet now he was fading away, perhaps forever.

Cheshire's grin lasted longer than the rest of him but soon that too disappeared, pausing to mouth in a silent and ghoulish way the word "Run!"

Alice had gained hope and wisdom from Cheshire but this didn't stop her from feeling alone and scared. She didn't want to die here. She turned her head towards the irate crowd, which was approaching fast. Some of them had begun to run and she could plainly hear her name being called in anger.

Suddenly, from the fields either side of the road, creatures of all shapes and sizes began to appear and block the way forward. Alice could make out some of the larger animals - sheep, cows and pigs – as well as flocks of birds. They seemed to be confronting the army of townsfolk, who were forced to stop in their tracks.

A ringing sound made Alice look down and through her tears she saw the familiar sight of a black telephone. The face of the telephone was ghostly white and its digits formed a troubled look. Alice picked up the receiver immediately and held it to her head.

"Alice?"

"Cheshire? Where are you? I thought you had gone for good."

"I have. I'm in a wonderful place. It's everything I hoped it would be. Believe me. But listen, you don't have much time. You have to get off the road before the mob gets there. They are angry at you."

"Why? What have I done?"

"It's not what you've done, it's what you stand for. Jackson MacDonald was wrong. It's not only what you do in your life, it's what the people in power think you have done and how much they influence what other people think you have done.

"Jackson told you he had hidden the coins he collected from people, didn't he? Well, the Gang Green has apparently got hold of them. Thousands of them. With all the notes burnt, the value of coins has risen so fast, that as soon as the Gang Green released the coins back into circulation, people did anything to get their hands on them. So it really is true: look after the pennies and the pounds will look after themselves.

"Egged on by the Gang Green, the people of Banbury have forgotten all the good they heard about Jackson and are back lusting for wealth. Money is all they really care about. That's all they ever really cared about. Jackson is apparently now an inmate himself at Sweatlands, unable to leave. The Gang Green have convinced the people that Jackson kidnapped their children, stole their money to build his own fortune and that you helped him do that by enlisting an army of animals to protect him."

"But that's ridiculous."

"It doesn't matter what you think. Or what the truth is. It's what they think that counts. You remember that you told Humphrey Dunfry to go back and let Mrs MacDonald's animals go free? Well, he did just that. With the help of the animals you befriended, they are stirring up all the other animals to stand up to oppression. They're staging a revolt in your name."

"Oh no! What have I done?"

"It doesn't matter. All that matters to you is that you need to run. Get off the road. Now!"

It was so unfair. Everything Jackson had done and tried to do had been undone in the blink of an eye. Worse still, he was now a prisoner in Sweatlands, a place infinitely more daunting than the Council House, with little chance of ever seeing Polly again. How could people be so fickle? The townsfolk of Banbury had heard Mayor Jackson's story as Polly broadcast it across the market square and had learned how the Gang Green was behind all the greed and corruption. They had even thanked Alice. Yet for the sake of a few coins each, they had swallowed the lies of the Gang Green and were now out for her blood.

She looked back down the road and saw scuffles had broken out between the animals and the people. After trying in vain to reason with the townsfolk, the animals were now barring their way. But the people were incensed and most of the animals old and weak.

It pained Alice to see two old sheep fall beneath blows from sticks and cudgels. A few dogs dived into the fracas, led perhaps by Colonel Pavlov, but they were brushed aside by the sheer size and power of the mob. A murder of crows whirled above as people waving sticks tried to knock them out of the sky. A part of Alice wanted to run back and help them but she knew it was their choice to be there. Their right.

Animals of all kinds, wild and domesticated, emerged from the undergrowth. Alice was sure Chester would be among them. Perhaps Kevin and possibly even Jeremiah (albeit a little behind the others). Insects too swarmed into the fray. She watched as creatures threw themselves to destruction.

"I'll always be with you, Alice."

"Who are you really, Cheshire?"

There was a short pause. "Some rules one simply can't break. Not even in Wonderland. Goodbye, Alice."

Alice handed the receiver back to the telephone, which broke its silence to scream just one word. "Run!"

With a quick look at the advancing throng, Alice removed her shoes and stepped off the road and onto the sand. If she had been expecting some magical shift in the world she would have been disappointed. The only thing that happened was that her feet sunk into the soft, hot beach. She was still very much in Wonderland.

A rusty metal knife, thrown by one of the crowd, clattered and skidded to a halt on the road nearby. Alice knew she had to get farther away and fast. She tried to run across the beach, pumping her legs up and down with all her might, but the deep sand slowed her progress. The fighting had now reached the end of the road. Soon they would be upon her.

She looked towards the sea as if to ask the waves for help and caught sight of a girl standing by the water's edge. It was Mary. How she had got there Alice had no idea. She was waving at Alice, not frantically but in a calm, friendly manner, as if she couldn't see the pandemonium behind. Alice could clearly hear cries of "Traitor!" and "Charlatan!" coming from the mouths of the ringleaders as they reached the edge of the beach. She saw a man fall to his knees beneath a pack of hamsters and a woman trying to strangle a turkey. She spotted two Gang Green members barking orders to the townsfolk as they tried to swat a swarm of wasps away. *At least the children had been spared.*

There was nothing for it but to run to Mary and ask her if she knew the way out of Wonderland. Slowly but surely, Alice managed to cross the sand and reach Mary, who was still smiling, oblivious to the advancing army.

Perspiration streaked down Alice's face. She wiped it away then wiped her hands on her dirty yellow dress. As usual, Mary's clothes looked as though they had just been ironed and her hair freshly washed and curled.

"Hello Alice. I sometimes sell sea shells here by the seashore. Today, I came here to look for some for my garden but I found you. It's lovely to see you again."

"Mary! If you know, please tell me how I can leave Wonderland! The people of Banbury have turned against me. The animals are trying to stop them but they are being massacred. Unless I escape … well, who knows what will happen."

Mary continued to smile as she said calmly, "Don't you know, Alice? You can never leave Wonderland."

"What do you mean, I can't leave? Ever? Why?"

"Well, not without me, in any case. And I know you won't take me with you because you don't like me. So it appears you are to remain here and witness Wonderland's downfall."

Alice was confused. Why was Mary being so mean? Why did Mary need to come with her anyway? They hardly knew each other. It was true, Alice didn't much care for the precocious girl standing in front of her. She belittled others and at times was even spiteful. So yes, Mary was perhaps the last person Alice would choose to take with her. But it was clear she knew how Alice could return home. So if that meant taking Mary along, then so be it.

"You can come with me, Mary. Just tell me how we can escape."

"You have to accept me as a friend, Alice. Let me in. You can't say you'll take me if you don't really mean it. It doesn't work like that."

"I do mean it. You can come. Let's go!"

"Really? You'll take me with you?"

"Yes. But quickly now. Tell me what to do."

A small man brandishing an ugly wooden club stepped off the road and onto the sand. Seeing nothing bad had happened to him, a larger man wielding a metal spear joined him. A woman also stepped onto the sand and shouted, "She's over there. Let's get her!"

As Alice had done, the attackers struggled to cross the soft sand.

Meanwhile, Mary wanted proof of Alice's sincerity. "First, tell me why you don't like me."

Alice tried to contain her frustration.

"I do like you," said Alice between gritted teeth. "I just told you!" She was now telling an outright lie and it felt bad. Mary looked out to sea as though she had all the time in the world.

"Does it matter why I don't like you?" asked Alice.

Mary began humming the tune to "I had a little nut tree". Alice was out of time, so why pretend anymore?

"All right! All right! I don't like you. It's because you're arrogant and self-centred. You judge others and can't stand people who think or act differently to you. You don't seem to appreciate ..."

Mary stopped Alice by taking hold of her arms and facing her square on. "Yes Alice. I'm all those things and more. But *why* don't you like me? Last chance! *Why*!"

Alice thought for a moment, although she wouldn't really have needed to.

"Because you remind me of me. All the worst parts of me." Alice repeated what she had just said in her head and burst into tears. She didn't resist when Mary embraced her gently.

"Oh Alice. Don't you understand? I am you. I've never been anyone else. Didn't you ever wonder why Humphrey Dunfry thought your name was Mary? Or why Mrs MacDonald suspected you were me? Or why nobody talked to me at the market place or the Unfair? It was because they couldn't see me. I was never there. You silly sausage."

Alice frowned as she tried to come to terms with the fact that Mary was a creation of her own imagination. She stared into Mary's eyes and saw the truth in it. She had hated Mary at times. But it was not because Mary merely mirrored the worst characteristics of herself, it was because Mary actually was the worst traits of Alice personified. Had Alice known deep down all along?

But why had Mary been created? Had Wonderland removed the worst part of Alice to make it easier for her to help the land and its people? Honey catches more flies than vinegar, as Mrs M had said. *Well, that hadn't worked out too well*. More probably, it had wanted to show Alice some bitter truths about herself. Or had Alice herself fabricated Mary? Was this one of the "defence mechanisms" her mother had once accused her of? Whatever the reason, it was time for her to face up to reality and be whole again.

Suddenly, a short way along the beach, the sand shifted. The tall and lanky body of a black Eeler rose out of the ground and pointed its cruel barbed fingers towards Alice. Its face was lost in shadow but its intent was clear. Along the shoreline in both directions, other Eelers emerged from the sand, towering silently and menacingly over Alice, cutting off her only escape route.

The people of Banbury, still embroiled in their battle with the creatures, had by now crossed the beach and were spreading out to encircle Alice. There was blood and sand everywhere. Still the creatures fought bravely to keep off Alice's aggressors, biting, scratching and stinging every inch of bare skin they could find. Against all odds, they had managed to slow down the army of people and let Alice reach the seashore. Yet there were just too many people with too many weapons. It wouldn't be long before the townsfolk or the Eelers would be upon her.

Ignoring others around her, Alice took Mary's face in her hands and kissed her lightly but with all the love she could muster. Tears sprung into Mary's eyes and the annoying smirk she had worn from the outset softened into the warmest smile Alice had ever seen. No longer caring if the people of Banbury or the Eelers harmed her, Alice wrapped her arms around Mary in such a tight embrace that their bodies melted into each other. She knew neither of them were perfect but together they could be a better person. Whether destined to fall or survive, Alice would do so a whole person. To her surprise, she found she was smiling.

She turned and looked with new eyes at the seething mob that faced her. She was no longer scared of them. There was no anger. Not even when one of them scratched the skin on her forehead with the point of a spear and drew a few drops of blood. She felt pain yes, and even alarm. But most of all, she felt sorry for all the people and animals. Sorry for Wonderland. She knew that she could no longer help them. Perhaps she never had been able to.

At the sight of blood on Alice's yellow dress, the people of Banbury paused their fighting and glanced at one another as if to say, she is mortal, not magical; merely a young girl, not a false prophet. In their eyes she became an injured child, awaking in them long-forgotten emotions.

Then a large lady, who held a knife, spoke up from the crowd. She spoke in a quiet voice but it was heard by everyone.

"Seize her. Lock her up. And throw away the key," said Mrs MacDonald, the farmer's wife.

"But she's just a little girl," said a man in the crowd, who had lost his appetite for violence.

"I'm not a little girl," said Alice, smiling, but with conviction. *I am so much more.*

"That's right, you're not," said Mrs MacDonald to Alice. She turned to the crowd and shouted, "You heard her. She's guilty. She hates us. She stole our money, our children. She's the ringleader behind the attack of the animals. She thinks we're nothing but a dream and now she wants to escape, leaving Wonderland in chaos. Our only hope is to keep her here. Seize her! Lock her up! And throw away the key! Seize her! Lock her up! And throw away the key!"

When two members of the Gang Green took up the chant, it became a mantra for others to copy. There was no more fighting, but soon a hundred people bayed for Alice's capture.

"Seize her! Lock her up! And throw away the key!"

Calmly, with the confidence of knowing that no one would stop her, Alice turned away from her would-be captors and her allies and walked slowly to the sea's edge. The waves used the last of their power to lap at her toes. She kept going. The crowd grew silent again as no-one had expected her to do something as foolish as to walk into the sea. A distance grew between the crowd and Alice but no-one followed her.

It was as if every living creature in Wonderland had gathered on that beach. Waiting and watching in silence. If the Cheshire Cat was to be believed, then everyone was indeed there, as he claimed nothing else existed outside of what Alice could see. She cared for them, all of them, even Mrs MacDonald. But she was not responsible for them. As they were not responsible for her. She was only responsible for herself.

Cheshire was right. It was Alice's time. Everything was now about her and her alone. She was free to return home. Smiling, partly at the effect her indifference was having on the crowd, Alice walked further into the water. Frightened she may drown, the waves tried to return her to the beach but she carried on. They tried to knock her from her feet but she remained upright. They buffeted her body but she refused to go back. Deeper and deeper into the water she walked until it was chest-high. The swell rocked her to and fro yet she would not fall. At long last, she knew she was going in the right direction. Of that she was sure.

Just as Alice wondered whether to fill her lungs with air and hold her breath, the sea level began to drop. From her waist to her knees, then down to her ankles. The tide was retreating at an impossible pace, racing far out to sea, as if sucked up by Neptune himself. It left a hundred thousand fish beached and gasping for breath. The sight caused a tightness in her chest.

Whether spurred on by the sight of a free meal or the chance to capture Alice, the dark Eelers waded effortlessly across the muddy sand towards her, their barbed limbs ready to skewer her. Their fury and hunger blinded them. They had not sensed the change in Alice. Neither had they seen the giant wave on the horizon; the tsunami that had the power to wash away all that was wrong with Wonderland and cleanse it of its troubles. It raced towards the beach like a screaming banshee, like a steam train whistling louder than a hurricane.

People and animals alike stood and waited, covering their ears against the shrill of the wave. They felt the wind as it fled to stay ahead of the rising sea. Then they heard the low rumble as the body of water pounded the seabed in its path and spoke to Alice of what was to come.

"Why?" she asked the sea. "It doesn't make sense. I saved the animals on the train, only to see them grow old and abused by the people. Now they stand up for their rights, only to sacrifice themselves in battle. What's it all for?"

The sea roared more loudly and Alice replied.

"The people of Banbury rejected corruption only to welcome it back with open arms. And what of their children?"

The wind snatched words from the surf and told Alice that nothing and no-one was all good or all bad. Done with talking to mortals, the sea grew higher still. Alice understood that before such might, all life was equal. Her understanding freed her from any guilt about leaving the creatures of Wonderland behind.

As the wave neared, it climbed to an impossible height, casting the land into shadow. Alice breathed deeply and smiled as the wall of water rose above her. She marvelled at the mermaids, serpents and other fantastic creatures silhouetted against the blue sky behind. They called out to her.

"You may control yourself but you cannot control Wonderland."

She had summoned a power that could wash away Wonderland's sin. But at what cost to those that lived here? *Swings and roundabouts,* said a voice in her head. *The way of the world.*

Alice trembled in wonder before the land's one true power. Then she surrendered herself utterly to a force that humans never would and perhaps never should attempt to comprehend. As the towering, deafening wave engulfed her, she felt insignificant yet at one with the Wonderland; miniscule and gigantic, nowhere and everywhere. She knew that whatever happened to her next would be the right thing.

The wave took her body, her breath and her mind. It tossed her in a hundred directions, twisting her in as many positions. It stole her thoughts and emptied her soul of any feelings. And finally, it spat her out into the cold air.

Alice found herself on her hands and knees, among the small stones and shallow waters at the edge of the river. The sea, the beach and the shrill whistling in her ears had all evaporated, as had all the creatures and people of Wonderland. The weir gurgled quietly like the muffled sound of silver bells.

Alice wore her white dress again and her new red shoes lay waiting for her on the riverbank. The only thing she had appeared to bring back with her was a stinging sensation on her forehead, where a weapon, or possibly a rock, had grazed her skin.

The sun was sinking in the sky and Alice knew that she must get home before her parents came looking for her. After all, she still had to pack. It would be nice to see her family and she would make a point of visiting home often once she had moved to London.

And yet she sat for a few moments more on the riverbank, listening to the soft drone of the insects and the twittering of birds that chased them. She breathed in the last of a rare summer evening. Above the sounds of nature, she could just make out the faint whistle of a steam engine many miles away.

She wondered if the blue dragonfly hovering an arm's length away had fought for her in Wonderland. What an ally a dragon would have posed for her attackers. She laughed at the absurdity of it all. At the same time, she knew that she didn't have the ability to dream up everything in such perfect detail all by herself.

There had been no Jabberwocky. Or then it had taken the form of greed and corruption that had threatened the very fabric of Wonderland. Had there only ever been one outcome to the chaos? Was she nothing more than a pawn on a chess board? Not even a queen this time? *And is Wonderland being recreated anew as I sit here, wrapped up in my own thoughts?*

And what was she supposed to learn from her adventure? She had spent years asking that same question following her first visits to Wonderland and it had almost driven her mad. *I'm not about to repeat that experience!* She was wise enough to know that she could not fully comprehend any deeper meaning. What she did know was that this had either changed something inside her for good or it had not. Therefore, the best thing she could do was to be herself, whoever she now was, and get on with life. Take things (and people) as they came. Maybe be a little more tolerant. She gave a deep but contented sigh and concluded that she wouldn't have missed this adventure for the world.

Just two more minutes by the river, she whispered to Mary. Time slowed. They looked out over the water to the opposite bank. To where water boatmen skated through a forest of reeds. To where a shoal of fish below the water were getting hungry. To where the water cooled and became darker. If one took the time to look and listen, one could learn so much about the world. Even about oneself.

Eventually, Alice rose and wandered slowly back towards the house. Her world was one of peace and hope. At least for now. A smile played across her lips as her fingertips came into contact with a pebble-shaped sweet in the pocket of her dress. And a feather. And she remembered.

The end

INDEX OF NURSERY RHYMES

Most of the adventures that Alice has in this book come from children's nursery rhymes or the various historical theories behind them. This is a fascinating exercise in itself with scholars referring to a rich range of sources - Norse mythology, political satire, religious persecution, wars and capital punishment to name a few.

Just in case you didn't spot all the nursery rhymes, or have forgotten them, here are the first line(s) of the ones used. Please note, there are typically several versions to each nursery rhyme, so some you might know by different words.

One two three four five, once I caught a fish alive.
Mary Mary, quite contrary. How does your garden grow?
I had a little nut tree, nothing would it bear.
Bobby Shafto's gone to sea, silver buckles on his knee.
Old Mother Hubbard went to the cupboard, to give the poor doggie a bone.
Old MacDonald had a farm, E-I-E-I-O.
Jack and Jill went up the hill to fetch a pail of water.
Bye Baby Bunting. Daddy's gone a-hunting.
Rock-a-bye baby, in the treetop.

This little piggy went to market.

Ladybird, ladybird, fly away home.

Little-Bo Peep has lost her sheep.

Little Boy Blue, come blow your horn.

Three blind mice, three blind mice, see how they run.

Pussy cat, pussy cat, where have you been?

The three little kittens they lost their mittens.

Ding dong bell. Pussy's in the well.

The Queen of Hearts she made some tarts all on a summer's day.

Tom, Tom, the piper's son, stole a pig and away he run.

As I was going to St Ives, I met a man with seven wives.

Humpty Dumpty sat on a wall, Humpty Dumpty had a great fall.

Mary had a little lamb, its fleece was white as snow.

There was a crooked man and he walked a crooked mile.

Brother Jaques, Brother Jaques, are you sleeping?

Ride a cock-horse to Banbury Cross.

One for sorrow, two for joy.

Ring a Ring o'Roses, a pocket full of posies.

Baa Baa black sheep, have you any wool?

Simple Simon met a pieman, going to the fair.

Rub-a-dub-dub, three men in a tub, and who do you think they be?

Hickory Dickory Dock, the mouse ran up the clock.

To market, to market, to buy a fat pig. Home again, home again, jiggety-jig.

Polly put the kettle on, Polly put the kettle on.

Jack and Jill went up the hill to fetch a pail of water.

Doctor Foster went to Gloucester in a shower of rain.

Georgie Porgie pudding and pie. Kissed the girls and made them cry.

Girls and boys come out to play, the moon doth shine as bright as day.

Oh, the Grand Old Duke of York, he had ten thousand men.

Little Jack Horner sat in the corner, eating a Christmas pie.

Old King Cole was a merry old soul and a merry old soul was he.

Peter, Peter, pumpkin eater, had a wife but couldn't keep her.

Cock a doodle do! My dame has lost her shoe.

Goosey, Goosey Gander, where shall I wander?

Here we go gathering nuts in May/Here we go round the mulberry bush.

Pease pudding hot, Pease pudding cold.

Pat a cake, pat a cake, baker's man. Bake me a cake as fast as you can.

Do you know the muffin man, the muffin man, the muffin man.

Jack Sprat could eat no fat, his wife could eat no lean.

Diddle, diddle dumpling, my son John. Went to bed with his trousers on.

It's raining, it's pouring, the old man is snoring.

ABOUT THE AUTHOR

Having journeyed out of his own personal rabbit hole after a colourful career in corporate communications, David Stoneham is now pursuing his lifelong dream of writing fantasy. Rather like the heroine of this book, he finds himself drawn to the curious, the fantastic and the peculiar. This is his first novel to reach the finishing line.

Born in London, David grew up on the south coast of England and currently lives in the fens of Finland where he has one wife, two dogs and three children.

Printed in the United States
By Bookmasters